“I have something to

Jace started to explain, but Mackenzie whirled around to face him.

“Don’t.” She bristled, and her finger jabbed in his direction. “Just don’t.”

“You don’t even know what it is!”

“Is it about Wilder Ranch?” Her tone snapped as fast and furious as a snake’s strike.

“Nope.”

“Then I don’t want to hear it.” She mounted up—the equivalent of a kid placing their hands over their ears. “We should get back.”

He didn’t move.

“I’ve got things to do, Hawke.” The reins twitched in her hands. He’d made her uncomfortable. He wasn’t sure why that ignited a flicker of happy in his gut. Probably because it meant he still affected her.

“You know your way from here.” She turned her horse. “I’ll see you when you get back.”

And then she left him. Sitting in her dust, her canteen still in his hands, words dying on his tongue that had needed to be said for seven years.

Huh. So that was what that felt like.

Jill Lynn is a member of American Christian Fiction Writers and won the ACFW Genesis Contest in 2013. She has a bachelor's degree in communications from Bethel University. A native of Minnesota, Jill now lives in Colorado with her husband and two children. She's an avid reader of happily-ever-afters and a fan of grace, laughter and thrift stores. Connect with her at jill-lynn.com.

Books by Jill Lynn

Love Inspired

Colorado Grooms

The Rancher's Surprise Daughter
The Rancher's Unexpected Baby
The Bull Rider's Secret

Falling for Texas
Her Texas Family
Her Texas Cowboy

Visit the Author Profile page at Harlequin.com.

The Bull Rider's Secret

Jill Lynn

LOVE INSPIRED BOOKS

ISBN-13: 978-1-335-42901-8

The Bull Rider's Secret

This edition published by arrangement with Love Inspired Books.

www.Harlequin.com

Printed in U.S.A.

My little children, let us not love in word, neither in tongue; but in deed and in truth.

—*1 John* 3:18

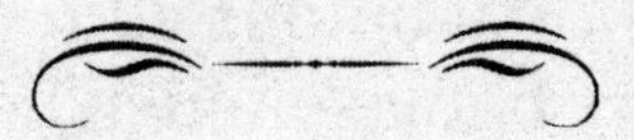

To my siblings—I'm thankful for your support and encouragement.

To Lost Valley Guest Ranch—A huge thank-you for your contributions to this series.

To Shana Asaro—Thank you for being a consistently fabulous editor. You make every book so much better.

And to everyone at Love Inspired—You're the best team, and I'm so glad to work with you.

Chapter One

Mackenzie Wilder didn't want to kill her brother in the true sense, just in the what-were-you-thinking, cartoon-wringing-of-the-neck sense. He'd gone and hired someone to help run the guest ranch for the summer—which meant the person would be completely involved in every aspect of her professional life—without asking for her input.

Had Luc talked to Emma before hiring this person? Not that it mattered. Their sister's head was so in-the-clouds in love right now that she'd say yes to anything and not even know what she was responding to.

Mackenzie bounded down the lodge steps, the screen door giving a loud whine and *snap* behind her. One of the new college-aged girls on staff for the summer was heading inside.

"Hey, Bea, have you seen Luc?"

"Earlier this morning he was in his office." Her face went dreamy, eyebrows bobbing. "He had some man candy with him, too." *Great.* Her brother had hired some young buckaroo who would have all of the female staff members sighing, swooning and requiring fainting couches all summer.

Maybe a what-were-you-thinking slug *was* in order.

"I just checked there, so now I'm headed to the barn. If you run into him, would you let him know I'm looking for him?"

If the man would just pick up his phone or respond to the texts she'd sent, Mackenzie wouldn't be on this scavenger hunt.

"Sure." Bea's short raven hair shifted with her perky nod.

"Thanks." Mackenzie's boots crunched

across the parched asparagus-colored grass, the short walk doing nothing to calm her frustration. When she stepped inside the barn, it took her a minute to adjust to the lack of light. She heard her brother before she saw him and followed his voice. He was talking to Boone, one of the new staff members—almost all of them could be labeled that this summer. And the timing for the turnover couldn't be worse.

Usually they had at least a few veteran staff return for the summer. Ones who could lead and train the more transitional summer help. But this year, everyone seasoned had moved on to greener pastures. Which was why she and Luc had hoped to hire someone to work with them—or at least closely under their direction. Especially with Luc and his wife, Cate, expecting twin girls in July.

Luc finished his conversation, and Boone headed outside. Mackenzie waited for him to be out of hearing range before she laid into Luc.

"Tell me your hey-I-hired-someone text

that I missed earlier this morning was a joke."

Luc scrubbed a hand through his short light brown hair, a grimace taking over his face. She was two inches taller than him, but he had her in brawn. Tall and straight, with muscles and barely existent curves, Mackenzie had accepted her body—or lack thereof—long ago.

"Nope. Not a joke. You know how much we need someone. And when I came across the right person yesterday, I snagged him." His hands went up like he was placating a skittish horse. "I know you're mad. Or I assume you are, but please trust me on this. Summer is completely stressing me out with the twins coming. We have no idea what that will look like, and I need to be available for them, for Cate."

"I get all of that." Mackenzie's rigid body kicked down a notch. "And of course we planned to hire someone, but I didn't think you'd go and do it without me."

"It just...happened." Luc leaned back against the workbench. "You know how hard it's been to find someone who's the right fit. And now summer season is here. We should have hired this person weeks ago. So, when I found a match, I jumped on it. I wasn't trying to overstep. I just—" his arms shot up in a helpless gesture "—feel better knowing we've got extra enforcements. Another lead. Someone who can handle the shooting range and staff and guests."

And how do you know this person can do all of those things? Do they have any experience?

But Mackenzie knew experience itself was overrated. What mattered was leadership and customer-service skills. If someone could handle a horse and interact well with staff and guests, they could be trained.

She slid her tongue between her teeth to trap it. To keep from continuing her tirade. Luc normally didn't pull stunts like this. But the babies had him all twitterpated. She could probably extend some grace. This time. And if Luc liked this new guy, she probably would, too. They thought alike. Had that twin connection that tethered her to him.

"Okay." She tried to get okay with her *okay*. "So, who is it?"

"Me." That voice.

It came from behind her, and she whirled to face it. *Him*. Jace Hawke. He stood just inside the open barn door, holding a saddle, sunshine outlining his silhouette like he was some sort of gift from above.

What? Impossible. Luc would never have hired her high school boyfriend. The ex who had turned her heart from mushy soft to solid boulder.

With his cowboy hat on, Mackenzie couldn't tell if she was still taller than Jace by a quarter of an inch. Yes—they'd measured back when they'd been young and in love. Before he'd trampled her to smithereens.

She straightened her shoulders, wanting to use every advantage when it came to him. Wishing she were a giant and she could squash him like a bug, then flick him out of the barn.

"Kenzie Rae." He nodded in greeting. As if they were old friends, without a mountain range of hurt between them.

He'd always called her that. Like he'd trademarked it. Owned it. Owned her, really.

And he'd always had an irritating drawl.

Well, in high school it hadn't been irritating. Back then it had curled into her, deep and warm and mesmerizing. She'd been starry-eyed over him. For two and a half years they'd dated. And he'd taken off, leaving her a note? A stupid, worthless note.

Emma's fiancé was always surprising her with notes, and she thought it was romantic. The girl went all swoony over the gesture. But not Mackenzie. Notes were cop-outs. Used when someone didn't have the guts to say something to your face.

Jace's jeans and boots and blue button-up shirt fitted him like a softened ball glove, outlining all of those I-left-you-to-go-ride-bulls muscles he'd accumulated over the years. And the same quiet confidence oozed from him.

The kind that destroyed everything in its wake. That told lies and then turned tail and ran.

"I'll store my saddle. Give you two a minute." He spoke to Luc, eyes toggling back to her before he strode toward the saddle room.

To store his saddle.

Because he was planning to stick around. Because Luc had hired him.

Seriously? Was she smack dab in the middle of a nightmare? Mackenzie slammed her eyelids closed. *He's not here. He's not here. I'm having a bad dream. I just need to wake up and then...* She peeked just as Jace disappeared through the saddle-room door. *He'll still be here.*

"You're playing me, right?" She held her brother's gaze. Glued herself there until he gave an answer as to why he'd do this to her.

His mouth was slightly ajar, as if he'd

just been declared at fault in a deadly accident. “I didn’t know it was like that. I didn’t realize… I thought the two of you ended on good terms.”

Because that was the story she’d spun the summer after graduation. Jace had left town to chase his dream and ride bulls… and she’d been all for it.

That had been so much easier to say than the truth: *he left me a note and took off. He never said goodbye. He destroyed me.*

Those weren’t phrases Mackenzie let into her vocabulary. Ever. And she’d worked incredibly hard to not let anyone—especially her twin—know how much Jace’s leaving had hurt her.

Turns out her efforts had worked.

“I ran into Jace in town last night, and we got to talking. He’s good with animals and people. He knows cattle roping, team penning, steer wrestling. He can teach the other wranglers some new competitions. The guests would love it. I thought he’d be a perfect fit.” Luc’s shoulder lift said, *I’m sorry* and *I didn’t know*, all rolled into one pathetic package that tugged on her sympathies.

Oh, Luc.

She understood why he'd hired Jace without talking to her first: the desperation he felt with twins on the way during their busiest time of year. But what was Jace even doing in town?

Why wasn't he off riding bulls? He couldn't need money, could he? Rodeoing would pay him far more than they ever could. And she'd followed enough of his career to know he'd been successful. Up until about three years ago, when she'd decided she couldn't handle it anymore and had to cut him loose. To not know what was going on with him. How he was faring. Not that Mackenzie ever planned to admit any of that.

Luc groaned. "I practically begged him to help us out for the summer."

Which translated in Luc-speak to "How can I go back on that? I can't unhire him."

Ugh. Her brother was her soft spot. Her

best friend. And he was destroying her right now.

"When were you planning to share all of this with me? After he'd been working here for two weeks?" Mackenzie detested the tremor lacing her questions, even if it was so slight, Luc probably didn't catch it. She didn't do shaky. Or nervous.

She did strong and unbreakable.

Except when it came to Jace Hawke.

"I called you twice last night and you didn't answer."

She'd fallen asleep on the couch. As usual.

"So then I sent you a text this morning."

"I was on a phone call." Their white-water rafting supplier had raised prices on this year's equipment without letting them know. She'd been negotiating for the sake of their business. *You're welcome.*

Jace cleared his throat, announcing his arrival as he exited the saddle room. Of course it hadn't taken him that long to store his saddle. He'd been giving them space. But the man couldn't stay in there forever, and that was how long it would take for Mackenzie and Luc to work this out.

Jace crossed to stand next to Luc. Like the two of them were a team in gym class Mackenzie wasn't invited to play on. He wrenched his hat from his head in a contrite gesture she didn't believe for a millisecond, sending honey-brown hair loping across his forehead.

"Luc." Bea popped her head into the barn. "Ruby took a tumble and scraped up her leg. She's screaming for you or Cate."

"Coming." Luc strode toward the exit, slowing as he passed her. "We'll talk more," he said for her ears only. "Just... behave yourself. Please."

Well. If he wanted results like that, he shouldn't leave her with the enemy.

But then again, he'd *hired* the enemy.

Whoo-ee. The amount of loathing streaming from Mackenzie was enough to heat the town of Westbend in the dead of winter.

Jace hadn't forgotten what a powerful force the woman was, but over time the memory of her had softened. He'd remembered all of the good. Had clung to it. But there was nothing muted about the live and in-person version of Kenzie Rae. She practically vibrated with intensity.

Looked like she hadn't forgiven and forgotten with time. Hadn't decided that him up and leaving town was no big deal. Bygones. All in the past.

But then, she didn't understand why he'd done it. And knowing her, she'd rather kick him in the shin than listen to any explanation he had to offer.

"What are you doing here?" The woman could sure make her voice hiss and spit fire when she put her mind to it.

Jace definitely preferred being on Mackenzie's good side. A position he'd ruefully given up seven years ago.

"Working. When I ran into Luc last night, he told me what you guys need for help and asked if I'd consider it." Taking a job at Wilder Ranch was better than being worthless while his body healed enough for him to go back to riding bulls.

Jace had messed up so many parts of himself over the years that he couldn't remember what all had been broken or crushed. But this time had been the worst. He'd bruised his spleen and his ribs. Gotten pounded so badly in the head that he was currently rocking the concussion to top all concussions.

But none of that would have kept him from the sport he loved.

A broken riding arm had cinched his demise. His *temporary* demise.

Her eyes narrowed. "Why aren't you off riding bulls?"

He rolled up his shirtsleeve to give Kenzie a better view of his cast. Eight weeks casted and then some rehab. Maybe more, the doctor had said. Maybe less, Jace had thought.

Was that a flash of sympathy from Mackenzie? Maybe even concern? The whole thing passed so quickly, Jace couldn't be sure.

"I suppose I didn't notice your cast earlier because of the dark red haze of anger and annoyance at your very presence clouding my vision."

Jace laughed. He couldn't help it. She might hate him, but he didn't reciprocate the feeling.

"I've no doubt you've been injured before. Why'd you come home this time?"

"My mom's not doing well." Her emphysema had worsened over the last few months, but she was still working two jobs. Taking medicine and pretending that the disease wasn't killing her. The woman wouldn't slow down. Jace could appreciate that, but he also hoped to convince her to give herself at least the chance for more time.

But he wouldn't have taken a break from bull riding just for that. He wasn't sure what that said about him. The injuries had forced him out. For now. And not one part of him wanted to admit to Mackenzie that his body was falling apart on his watch.

"I..." Her gaze softened. "I'm sorry to hear that about your mom."

"Thanks." The woman might be mad

enough to breathe fire, but she was still concerned about his mother. Jace appreciated that.

"You know what I'm really asking." Her words clipped out—bitter, heavy and dripping with suppressed frustration. "Why are you *here*?" Translation: "Why are you at Wilder Ranch? *My* ranch."

Because I have to work. Jace couldn't handle inactivity. Laziness. Ever since he'd been fifteen and made a decision he was still paying for. He refused to sit around this summer, while he healed… And no one else was going to offer him a job that would interest him in the least for such a short amount of time. Plus Wilder Ranch—and Mackenzie's family—had been a haven for him during the worst time in his life. If this place needed him, Jace couldn't say no to that.

Even if Mackenzie wanted to drop a sledgehammer on his bare feet and then shove him across red-hot embers.

"Why not here?" His trite answer earned a flood of silent responses. First anger. So much that her cheeks turned a distracting shade of pink. The pop of color highlighted her striking features, rocking him like a gale-force wind. But before he could deal with his unwelcome surge of attraction, her look changed to resignation, then hurt. The last one didn't stick around long, but it was enough to *whop* him in the chest. To make his heart hiccup.

Jace had never wanted to hurt Mackenzie. Not in a million years. He'd tried talking to her about his plans. He *had* talked to her. She just hadn't listened.

Leaving her had been the hardest thing he'd ever done. He'd hated it. Had even hated himself after.

It had been about so much more than the two of them. It had been about his brother, Evan, who'd lost the chance to chase his dreams because of a stupid, lazy choice Jace had made.

So Jace had done it for him. He'd had to. There really hadn't been a choice.

But it was seven years too late for explanations, and Mackenzie would crush them under her boot if he offered any up.

"You can't do this job with a broken arm." Her chin jutted in challenge.

"Exactly what can't I do?"

"Ride a horse."

He chuckled at that silly idea, and she stiffened so quickly that he was shocked steam didn't shoot out of her ears. Jace really wasn't trying to provoke her, but the idea of a fractured arm keeping him from riding a horse when he still had one good one was ridiculous.

"My arm won't prevent me from doing this job, and you know it."

A strangled *argh* came from her. Sweet mercy, she was mesmerizing when she was angry. All alive and mad and sparking.

"Jace." His name on her lips shot a strange thrill through him. "Please don't do this." Gone was the burning fire. Now she was deflated. Edged with sharp steel—the deadly stab-you-through-the-heart kind. "I get that Luc thinks we need you.

And yes, we need someone. But *I* need it not to be you."

She packed a lot of punch into her spiel. And the fact that she'd shown him any kind of emotion—that she was practically pleading with him not to stay… Jace would like to grant her that wish. He really would.

But he couldn't. Because he needed this ranch. And this place needed him back.

It would be the perfect situation if so much hadn't gone wrong between him and Mackenzie.

"I'm sorry. But I can't."

"Can't? Or won't?" Her arms crossed over her Wilder Ranch–logoed shirt, forming a protective barrier, and a scowl marred her steal-his-oxygen features. Man, she was gorgeous. Tall, long and strong, with petite curves. Jeans that hugged her. Worn boots. She was—had always been—a walking ad for all things casual and country and mind-numbing. She hardly ever wore makeup. Didn't need it. And her wild dark blond hair had most certainly air-dried into those relaxed waves, because she would never take the time to blow-dry it or spend more than five minutes in front of a mirror.

And yet she could take down most of the guys Jace knew with just one piercing glance from those gray eyes of hers. They weren't blue. That was too simple of a description. They were storm-cloud eyes, so striking and unusual he'd yet to find another pair that had rendered him as helpless as hers did.

"Won't." She was already upset with him. He might as well fuel it. At least that would keep him from thinking she'd ever forgive him for leaving. From thinking that there could ever be a second chance between them.

Not that he wanted one. Because once Jace got the all clear to go back to rodeoing—despite the doctor's recent warning that he shouldn't be doing anything of the sort—he'd be long gone again.

Chapter Two

"I'm not doing it. I'm not training him." Mackenzie winced at her petulant declaration, which was reminiscent of the tone her four-year-old niece, Ruby, used when she threw a fit. When the girl wanted to watch a show *right now.* And then usually ended up losing that very privilege because of her attitude.

Luc shook his head, his sigh long and ranking at a ten on the what-am-I-going-to-do-with-you scale.

The two of them sat on the corral railing as a gorgeous Colorado sunset showed off with pink-and-orange streaks kissing the mountains, and the cool air offered a respite from the warm late-spring day.

They'd been watching, encouraging and directing as the wranglers had practiced for one of the nightly performances they'd put on once the guests arrived. The first week might be rough, but it would come together.

It always did.

Ever since she'd been a little girl, Mackenzie had loved everything about Wilder Ranch. The guests who came back year after year. The wide-open land. The hot springs, the fishing, the shooting, the short drive to glorious, unfettered white-water rafting. This place just made sense to her.

Unlike Luc, she'd never had to run off for a time to figure out that this was where she wanted to be. She understood now why Luc had gone to Denver the fall after they'd graduated high school. But at the time she couldn't have said anything of the sort.

After Luc's return to the ranch, when their parents had decided to move to a different climate for their mom's health, it had been a no-brainer that Mackenzie would stay and run the ranch with her siblings.

She'd never struggled with being here—until Jace's appearance earlier today.

"If I give in on him staying..." Mackenzie still didn't say his name. Couldn't. "Then I should at least not have to train him."

If. Mackenzie clung to the word even though that option was slipping through her fingers. Luc was as sturdy and dependable as tree roots that sank into the ground and held tight for centuries. He wouldn't renege. If he'd hired Jace, Mackenzie didn't have much hope of upending that offer.

But maybe she could avoid him. Not run away—that was too weak. But just happen to never work anywhere near him for the rest of the summer.

That sort of impossibleness.

Please, please, please.

"Okay. I will. But then you have to do my job."

She groaned. She loathed bookwork. Paperwork. Life-sucking monsters. "I can't believe you hired my ex." That title was too formal. "My high school boyfriend." That was a little better.

"I really didn't know things ended badly between you, or I wouldn't have. I can't believe you hid that from me."

Mackenzie didn't defend her actions, because what he'd said was true. And hiding things from Luc was no easy task.

"I always just thought he'd left to ride bulls," her brother continued. "I didn't know you were so angry at him about it."

Ouch. That smarted. "He left—" she swallowed, but it didn't add any moisture to her mouth, which felt as if she'd been hiking for a week without provisions "—in a jerky way. Things didn't end well."

And then you left me, too.

Mackenzie hadn't admitted to anyone how hurtful Jace's departure had been. She was supposed to be strong, tough, solid—physically, yes. But also mentally. Emotionally. And Jace's disappearance had cut so deep, she'd been petrified that she'd never recover.

And then, before she'd even had a chance to begin doing exactly that, Luc had decided to move to Denver.

Both of them had abandoned her. It wasn't the first time Mackenzie had been left behind. Nor, she doubted, would it be the last.

"My to-do list is long right now. There's a stack on my desk of insurance issues and bills. Plus we're having a website problem, so I need to call about that."

"Can a person be allergic to paperwork?" Mackenzie rubbed a hand across the front of her neck. "I think my throat's closing off."

Luc snorted.

A fresh chill skimmed along Mackenzie's arms as the quiet night expanded with chattering crickets and a slight breeze rustling new leaves.

"You know you'll probably have to help out some when the babies come. I mean, I'm still planning to work, but Cate will need me. I promised her that she wouldn't be on her own."

This time. Mackenzie clenched her jaw. She'd gotten over what Cate had done in not telling Luc about Ruby until the girl was three years old. And it wasn't even her business. Cate was really great. Luc loved her—that much was clear. And Mackenzie had gotten on board. Had forgiven her now sister-in-law for doing what she had done.

But Mackenzie was still protective of Luc. She always had been. When they were kids and he'd needed open-heart surgery, it had felt like she was on that operating table with him. Like she was being cut open, too.

Luc had always been her person. When he'd left the ranch, she'd been so mad. Mostly because she'd missed him so much. The day he'd decided to come home, his truck kicking up dust down the long ranch drive, it was as if she'd been taken off life support and her lungs had kicked into functioning mode again.

Now that Luc had a family, she still

missed him sometimes. It only made sense that he'd spend most of his time with them. And yeah, she saw him plenty because they worked together. But he'd been her closest friend for most of her life. She wasn't girlie. Didn't have any desire to go shopping with Emma and Cate when they went on one of their marathon trips—she just…wasn't built that way. Mackenzie had always hung out with the boys. She and Luc had shared friends. And pathetically, now that he had a life and she didn't, she missed her brother. A mortifying confession she'd go to her grave denying.

"Hopefully the babies will sleep like champs and not fuss, but there's no guarantee of that. I missed so much with Ruby, and I just can't do that this time."

Knife to the heart. Luc was right, and she should jump on the supportive-sister bandwagon and…support him. "Do you have to be so logical? Can't you take a day off once in a while?"

He laughed. "You're usually right there

with me. But Jace has you messed up. I've never seen you so…shaken over a guy."

Ho-boy. She didn't like that description of her one bit. She was acting like a train wreck.

Mackenzie had to pull herself together and stop letting it show how much Jace got under her skin.

And really, why should he have that much of an impact on her? It had been so many years since he'd hightailed it out of town that she should be long over these jumbled, intrusive feelings.

Mackenzie didn't think about Jace all of the time anymore. Not like she had when he'd first run away.

But she did have questions. Like, why had he called her the week after he'd left? And the next week, too? Two phone calls, no messages.

She'd been consumed by what she would do if she happened to catch his call. Would she answer or not?

Turned out her uncertainties hadn't mattered, because the attempts to reach her had stopped.

Maybe Mackenzie's issues were more with things left unsaid—undone—than the fact that she was still affected by Jace.

Maybe she was truly over him, but those whys remained.

If that were the case, she'd feel like far less of an idiot. Because that would mean she wasn't still hung up on *him*. Just on how things had ended.

"I'll train him."

Luc's head cocked to one side, as he studied her, analyzing her sudden change of mind.

"What? I can do it and be professional." *I think.*

Mackenzie had to prove to herself that she could handle being around Jace without letting him affect her. Had to prove that he didn't still have a hold on her.

And there was a secondary hidden agenda to her offer. If Luc were to train Jace, he'd be so thorough that Jace would be able to run the guest ranch himself in a week's time. But if Mackenzie trained him…she could brush over things. Hurry along. It wasn't like she had a bunch of extra time on her hands anyway.

Despite Luc's confidence in Jace, the man had no idea what he was doing. He'd fail before long, and then he'd leave on his own.

Just because she refused to let Jace affect her anymore didn't mean she wanted him anywhere near her or involved in her life.

So yes, Mackenzie would train him. Because the faster he failed, the faster he'd go away.

Jace would figure out how to make himself useful this summer if it killed him.

And this staff meeting might do exactly that.

Well, not the meeting so much as the ice-cold gusts rolling off Mackenzie. The ones giving him frostbite despite the sunny, seventy-degree weather outside.

"Jace will be helping out this summer." Mackenzie spoke to the staff, who had gathered. The first full-week summer guests arrived tomorrow, and the group had been wrapping up last-minute details. "Especially with Luc and Cate expecting the babies. We're not sure how all of that will go. So..." Mackenzie swallowed. Took about twenty years to continue. "Let's welcome him."

Let's. Meaning everyone except for her. Mackenzie might be spouting one thing, but her body language said, *Pack up and get out of here.*

Jace had hoped that she'd calm down overnight and accept that he was planning to stick around for a bit. He'd thought maybe they could actually forget the past and get along for the summer. But if anything, Mackenzie was even chillier than she'd first been. At least yesterday she'd showed some emotion, asking him not to stay. But now? It was like she'd built a wall between them.

She'd offered him a clipped "good morning" earlier, when she'd told him which room in the guys' lodging would be his and tossed him a key, but other than that, she'd avoided him as if he were a pest or a varmint or some kind of beauty product that she wouldn't touch with a ten-foot pole.

And really, Jace didn't expect anything else from her. He'd been a jerk leaving the way he had. Yes, he'd loved her. But he'd also *had* to go. The pull had been so strong, it hadn't been a real choice. Not when his brother's dream had become unattainable for him. Not when he'd told Jace to go, to live it for him.

Mackenzie dismissed the meeting, and the staff dispersed, their conversations light.

"I'm Boone. Good to have you here." A young man offered his hand, and Jace shook it. The staffer didn't look a day over sixteen. Was it even legal for him to work here at that age? Or perhaps he was still growing into his body. Either way, Jace didn't plan to ask for details. When Luc had said they were low on veteran staff this summer, he hadn't been exaggerating.

Everyone seemed so young. Like puppies. No wonder they'd wanted to hire a lead. Jace might not have experience working a dude ranch, but he knew horses and livestock and pieces of ranching from working one during the summers in high school. People, he could do—he'd always had a way with the human species. So maybe this whole idea wasn't so crazy after all.

"I follow bull riding. Saw a clip of the Widow Maker ride."

Just the name of the bull caused Jace to break out in a flu-like sweat.

He'd watched the ride after the fact… He'd had to see it to know what had happened to him, because he didn't remember any of it. His body had been tossed and trampled like a rag doll in a terrorizing toddler's hands.

It was amazing he'd survived the ordeal. He'd only watched the video once, and that had been enough.

"That was quite the ride."

"You can say that again. You ride?"

"No. Did some mutton busting when I was younger, but nothing since."

"You could always get back to it." Possibly. Maybe. Though the kid was scrawny. "Let me know if you ever need any lessons."

Boone grinned. "Not sure I'm willing to risk my life like that, but I'll keep it in mind." After a nod, he took off.

A girl—maybe around nineteen or twenty—was talking to Mackenzie, and their conversation was quiet. Everything about the girl was thin. Her body. The hair barely filling out her ponytail. Was she okay? It looked like the world had chewed her up and spit her back out. In contrast, Mackenzie glowed with health and strength.

Jace wasn't trying to overhear, but their chat filtered in his direction. The girl was asking for an advance on her paycheck.

Mackenzie nodded, listening. "I'll talk to Luc and Emma, and we'll let you know." She squeezed the girl's arm in a reassuring gesture, and then the little mouse scampered off.

Mackenzie was supposed to train him today. At least that was what Luc had said. Jace wasn't sure how that would work when she was treating him like a rat in the gutter, but he was game if she was.

The day was sure to be a barrel of fun. Especially since his head was teetering on the edge of a cliff, deciding, without his input, whether to calm down or throw a fit.

Which could be because he'd had a hard time falling asleep last night. Jace wasn't sure which had caused that symptom—the concussion or the woman in front of him. It was a toss-up. Thoughts of Mackenzie—of the relationship they'd once had—had been resurrected like vivid movies. To the point that he'd finally slept and dreamed about her. Dreamed that he'd stayed in Westbend. That she didn't hate him.

Things that had consumed his mind when he'd first left to ride bulls and had holed up in an apartment with a few other guys in Billings. And then the rodeo had fully distracted him. And finally, finally the part of him that had been screaming that he'd made a mistake had lightened up. Quieted.

Until now—until seeing Mackenzie again. The need to work, to not spend his days lazing around, might not be worth this headache. And yet the challenge of something new, of helping out Luc and Mackenzie and Emma, still pulled at him.

Jace wasn't ready to give up a qualified ride yet, even though that was probably exactly what Mackenzie hoped and prayed he would do.

But since Jace's prayers were the opposite, that left them in a spiritual tug-of-war. Because, as far as Jace knew, God didn't pick sides. He loved both of them. And the Man upstairs was going to have to work this out. Because Jace didn't see Mackenzie calling a truce anytime soon.

"Well." Mackenzie shuffled papers on the table, which held her attention like her favorite pair of boots. Finally she glanced up, regarding him with as much contempt as she might a door-to-door salesman peddling high-priced skin-care products. "I should show you the trails. You might lead some rides, and either way you'll need to know where the groups are in case of an emergency."

"Don't I already know them?" They'd been all over this land together in high school. Had ridden more times than he could count.

Jace had preferred time with Mackenzie over the agony of watching his brother try to figure out how to live after losing part of his leg. It had been pretty awful around his house for a while. When Jace had been eleven, their father had been killed in a bar brawl. Drinking had always been his most important relationship, and his presence in their lives before that had been sporadic. Four years later Evan's foot and part of his leg had been amputated because of a lawn-mower accident. Mom had struggled—working constantly to support them and pay for Evan's medical bills.

Jace had escaped to Wilder Ranch all of

the time in high school. Kenzie Rae had been his escape. The truth of that made every bruised, broken and sprained muscle or bone he'd experienced riding bulls roar back into existence.

"You'll know some. But a few are new." She strode to the door and then paused inside the frame, tapping the toe of her boot with impatience when he didn't immediately sprint after her. "You coming?"

"Right behind you."

And that was how it was on the trail, too. Mackenzie led. Jace followed. There was no riding next to each other. No conversation.

Only him trying—and failing—not to notice everything about her. Being relegated to the back seat on the ride gave him the chance to drink her in, to catalog the slight changes that had come with time. Jace had left a girl behind and had come back to find a woman. One who didn't need him. Didn't want him. Didn't know why he'd done what he'd done.

With her dark blond hair slipped through

the back of a baseball cap, and wearing a simple gray V-necked T-shirt, jeans and boots, Mackenzie turned casual into a heap of trouble.

They rode enough of the new trails that he gathered what he needed to know between her directions and the hand-drawn map she'd tucked into her back pocket.

When they reached a wide, smooth path that carved through open pasture, she didn't give him even the slightest heads-up before urging her horse into an all-out gallop.

The smart thing to do would be to let her ride. Enjoy the view. But Jace had never been one to take the easier road.

He nudged his horse into action.

If he'd thought Mackenzie was distracting earlier, seeing her fly wasn't helping matters.

The flat-out run was worth it—gave him a hint of that risking-it-all feeling—but by the time Mackenzie slowed Buttercup and eased her back into the trees, the dull ache in Jace's head had ramped up from barely noticeable to jet-engine-roar levels. And his ribs were on fire.

Probably not his best move, since he was supposed to be taking it easy. But not joining Mackenzie would have been painful in other ways. For a few seconds he'd felt young and free. Like they still had their whole futures ahead of them. He missed that, especially now. If Jace couldn't go back to rodeoing, what would he do with himself?

He'd never been any good at school. Or any job other than the one currently dangling out of his reach.

"You weren't lying when you said you could ride with one arm." Mackenzie tossed the comment/compliment over her shoulder as they reached the hot springs and she dismounted. It registered in Jace's chest, warm and surprising. *Getting ahead of yourself, Hawke. She didn't say she was crazy in love with you, just that you could handle a horse.*

Jace mimicked her dismount, needing a second to steady the wavelike motions crashing through his noggin. He'd give a hefty sum of money for an ice pack to press against his wailing ribs, which were none too pleased with his recent activity.

Mackenzie must have realized her mistake in leading them to the hot springs, because her vision bounced from the water, to him, then back.

Yep, you sure did deliver us right back to the past.

They'd been out here plenty of times when they were young. Had stolen kisses in those very waters.

Back then she'd welcomed an advance from him. Even initiated.

Jace wobbled and managed to right himself while Mackenzie was thankfully looking in the other direction. He was far weaker than he should be, which only added to the angry rhythm inside his skull.

He hated being sidelined. Benched. Hated it even more that he didn't know when or if these concussion side effects would go away or get better.

The arm, the spleen, the ribs—none of

that bothered him, because he knew they'd heal. But his noggin had a mind of its own.

He dropped to sit on a rock in the shade and settled his head in his hands. He sensed Kenzie moving but didn't look up. And then a canteen appeared between his arms.

"Thanks." He took it, meeting those stormy eyes. She walked toward the hot springs as he drank. The water was cool, crisp and, if he wasn't mistaken, the faintest taste of her mint Chapstick still coated the lip. He plucked a pill out of his front pocket and shot it down before Mackenzie turned back in his direction.

She studied him as she neared, stopping about five feet away. Enough that he could feel her intense observation, but not so close that she actually stepped foot into his world, his space.

"You okay?"

"I'm fine. Just hot, I guess." He took another swig.

"Your arm hurting?"

He hadn't even thought about that slight discomfort today. "Nah. I'm good."

Except he wasn't.

Mackenzie was a deer in the forest. Still. Analyzing. Eyes morphing to slits. She'd have him figured out in two seconds flat if this kept up. And for some reason he didn't want her to. If she knew about the ribs or spleen, that would be fine. But his head felt too…personal. No one knew that Dr. Karvina had advised he quit riding.

I'm going to level with you, Jace. If this were me or one of my sons, I'd quit now. I can't tell you how many concussions you can survive without permanent damage. It's not worth the risk. I've seen too many lives taken or changed forever by this sport.

His doctor's advice haunted him. Concussions were a big deal these days. Last year a young rider had committed suicide after one too many. After his death, the autopsy had confirmed he had CTE, a terrible disease that came from repeat trauma to the brain.

Head injuries had messed with his moods, his memory, even his personality. Gunner's last hit had been a whopper though. But still, no one knew the exact number of concussions that would be okay. Or how many would push a guy over the edge. Ever since the young cowboy had taken his own life, the rules had gotten stricter for all of the riders. It was logical—Jace could admit that. But that didn't make it easy to think about losing everything.

Which was why so many guys still did what they wanted—still rode when they shouldn't.

And Jace understood that, too. He wasn't done riding. It was his life. His people. He'd done it for his brother, but it had become his, and he wasn't going to quit now.

And he certainly wasn't going to discuss any of this with Mackenzie. The woman who constantly wanted to kick him in the shins and then slug him.

Maybe he should just explain why he'd left. Get it all out in the open now. She could still hate him then, but at least she'd have answers.

"Kenzie Rae."

She'd begun pacing back toward the water but now whirled around.

"I have something to say—"

"Don't." She bristled, and her finger jabbed in his direction. "Just don't."

"You don't even know what it is!"

"Is it about Wilder Ranch?" Her tone snapped as fast and furious as a snake's strike.

"Nope."

"Then I don't want to hear it." She mounted up—the equivalent of a kid placing their hands over their ears. "We should get back."

He didn't move. Just glued himself to her until she called uncle and wrenched her gaze away.

"I've got things to do, Hawke." The reins twitched in her hands. He'd made her uncomfortable. He wasn't sure why that ignited a flicker of happiness in his gut. Probably because it meant he still affected her. And since she was under his skin like a chigger, yeah, that eased the sting a bit.

"You know your way from here." She turned her horse. "I'll see you when you get back."

And then she left him. Sitting in her dust, her canteen still in his hands, words dying on his tongue that had needed to be said for seven years.

Huh. So that was what that felt like.

Chapter Three

Seven days at the ranch, and nothing had changed.

Mackenzie still didn't want him here. And Jace still refused to go.

Though he was starting to doubt his decision. Kenzie's disdain for him was beginning to seep into the cracks of his confidence.

Should he give in and quit? Crash on his mom's couch for the next weeks or months, instead of his room at the ranch? Go absolutely crazy from boredom and live suffocated by the fear that he'd never heal and return to his career?

He just couldn't function that way. No

matter how much he'd like to not torment Mackenzie. Besides, he liked it here. Liked leading trail rides, the weather, the views, the wrangler competitions they entertained the guests with at night. Guest ranch life was busy—so full of people and staff and horses that his mind hadn't gotten bogged down with what-ifs about his injuries and the future.

Definitely not the worst job he'd had.

Except for the woman who hated him.

Oh, *hate* might be too big of a word for how Mackenzie felt about him. He was a pebble in her boot. An annoyance that she planned to ignore.

And then she approached the table where he was eating lunch with guests and other staffers and did exactly that.

She asked the guests how their day was going. She made sure to acknowledge each of the staff. And then she left the dining room. Didn't she realize that completely ignoring him was more noticeable than treating him like she did everyone else?

Jace popped up, cleared his dishes and

then chased after her. He caught sight of her in the lodge living room—an inviting place with high ceilings, comfortable furniture and a massive fireplace that begged for snowstorms and cold winter nights.

Mackenzie's hair was down today—long and wild, and bringing him back to high school and the memory of what it had felt like to thread his fingers through those waves and kiss that mouth that had once been receptive to his.

Even in her jeans and a simple Wilder polo, the woman could cause a freeway pileup. She had on turquoise boots today—the third different pair he'd seen her wear since he'd arrived at the ranch. Mackenzie had hated shopping back in high school. Her only girlie addiction had been boots. Apparently that infatuation had continued.

No guests occupied the lobby at the moment, so Jace called out to her, "Kenzie Rae."

She turned to face him, upset heating her cheeks. At his presence or the use of her nickname?

Either way she'd have to adjust.

He stopped in front of her, ignoring her obvious irritation at his interruption. "What do you need me to do tonight?"

Being that this was his first week, he was still learning the schedule. Mackenzie might not want him here, but while he was, he planned to do a good job of whatever they asked him to do.

The glint in her eyes was quick as a bullet and disappeared just as fast. "The square dance is tonight."

Huh. He wouldn't be much of a help with that.

"Why don't you lead it?"

Jace snorted. "Ha. Very funny." She didn't laugh, didn't join in. "Wait. You're serious?"

"Why not? Luc seems to think you're so qualified to be working here. Not that anyone asked me. So, if that's the case, you can be in charge tonight."

"So that's how you're going to play it? I don't have any idea how to square-dance. You know I'm a pathetic dancer." The only real rhythm he'd ever had was on a bull. When he'd competed on the weekends in high school, Mackenzie had always come to watch him ride when she hadn't been working herself. After, there'd often been a dance, a band, a crowd. A few times they'd attempted the steps, but never with much success. Once or twice he'd just held her. Held on as if his life had depended on it. On her. He supposed it had in a way. She'd been everything to him. The future he'd denied himself when he'd chased Evan's dreams.

"I haven't seen you in seven years, so I know nothing of the sort."

Silent accusations brimmed, and Jace understood them. Had she wondered what he was up to over the years? If he was dating anyone? Because he'd wondered those things about her. It would have destroyed him to find out she was in a relationship or married, even though he didn't have any right to her anymore.

"I didn't take you to be vindictive, Kenzie Rae." He dropped the name on purpose now, goading, a little of her anger seeping over to him.

"Really? Maybe *you* don't know *me* at all anymore. I'm not sure you knew me then either."

Sweet mercy. The woman's punches were fast and furious and vicious and deserved. Jace rubbed a hand over his certain-to-be-gaping chest wound before that same traitorous hand snaked out and latched onto her arm.

The heat between their skin sizzled as much as their rising irritation. "I knew everything about you back then and vice versa."

"The Jace I knew would never have left like you did."

There would be no closing the wound today. Not with Mackenzie hitting the same spot over and over again. "I tried to tell you." His voice dropped low, aching with remorse. "So many times. But the words always got stuck." He swallowed. "And when I did manage to get some of it out, you didn't listen."

For a split second she'd softened during his speech. Those mesmerizing eyes had notched down from bitter to curious, *tell me why* shooting from them. But at his *you didn't listen*, everything in her hardened and lit like fireworks.

"I'm not doing this." She shook his hand loose as if he were nothing more than dirt—or worse—hitching a ride on her boots. "This is exactly why I was so mad that Luc hired you. Wilder Ranch is my family business, Hawke. My life. And you're not in it anymore. As far as I'm concerned, your time here is strictly about work. I don't want to hear any of this. It's too late to make apologies…if that's even what you're doing. It's too late to try to blame me for what *you* did. So if you want to be here, figure out how to lead the square dance, because as your *boss*, that's what I'm directing you to do."

Before Mackenzie could take off or Jace could process his jumbled thoughts enough to respond, the screen door to the lodge opened and Emma walked inside. Thankfully it was her and not a guest. She was all sunshine in a yellow shirt, jeans and rain boots as she paused to study them—probably taking in their irritated body language or analyzing whatever she'd just overheard.

Emma bravely continued in their direction. "Everything okay in here?" A faint curve of her lips attempted to diffuse the negative energy that surely radiated from them.

Kenzie's gaze slit and slid from him to her sister. "We're great." Fake perkiness punctuated her answer. "Jace and I were just discussing his duties for tonight. And he was expressing how excited he is about them. I mean—" her sarcasm ramped up "—since this is the perfect place for him to work, and Luc seems to think he's so qualified, I thought I'd give him some more responsibility."

Vicious woman. Jace willed himself not to find her attractive in the middle of her feisty little speech.

It didn't work.

If Emma wasn't watching them like a

spectator at a UFC fight, Jace would seriously toy with the thought of kissing Mackenzie just to get her to stop spewing venom. An action that might very well leave him as messed up as stomping through a field of rattlesnakes.

"Of course. I'm happy to do anything I'm assigned." Square dance? Fine. He'd figure it out. Somehow. There had to be another staffer who had a clue about what to do.

Mackenzie's determination to boot him out of here only increased his resolve to stay. She should know better than to challenge him, to turn this into a competition. His whole livelihood depended on him besting a two-thousand-pound bull.

Emma's strangled sigh was filled with exasperation, and a tinge of remorse lit in Jace. He shouldn't have engaged with Mackenzie at all. Certainly not in the lodge lobby, where guests could walk through at any second of the day.

"Feel like you two could use a mediator. Or some workplace counseling. Is that a thing?" Emma beamed, finding her own joke amusing. Jace's lips twitched, because the idea of Mackenzie and him sitting on a couch, trying to figure out how to work together when she couldn't stand the sight of him, *was* funny, but he couldn't let Mackenzie win the third-grade angry-staring contest they'd somehow begun.

"Um, so…listen." Emma was made of velvet—a stark contrast to Mackenzie's most recent tone. "I need people to get along. I can't handle all of this." Her nose wrinkled, and she waved a hand, encompassing them. "What can I do to help you guys? Because I get the past mattering and all that. Trust me—I understand how much that affects things. But you two have to figure out how to work together and not do this—" another hand motion "—anywhere guests or staff can see you."

She was right, of course. But Jace had been trying. For the most part.

"Maybe we could schedule in special argument time after everyone else has signed off for the night. Or get up early and duke things out." Jace let the retort slip, hoping it might earn the faintest shadow of humor—like the old Mackenzie would have offered up.

New Mackenzie released a growl/wounded-animal screech of frustration. "Actually, Emma, the best scenario would be for Jace to realize he's not welcome at Wilder Ranch and leave."

Emma's mouth formed an O shape as Mackenzie made a U-turn and strode toward the front office, her boots pounding as strong and fierce as she was.

Attraction swallowed Jace up. Confounded woman.

"That is not true." Emma's light brown ponytail and silver hoop earrings bobbed back and forth with her shaking head. "Of course you're welcome here. You always have been. I'm sorry for her—"

"You don't need to apologize for Mackenzie. I'm not surprised. And I deserve everything she's throwing my way."

The woman only seemed to reserve direct hits for him. Jace had learned that the

Wilders had extended the paycheck advance to the girl asking for it. They were gracious like that. Even Mackenzie was. Just not with him.

"Oh, Jace." Emma softened. "It has been a long time. I was never sure exactly what happened between you two, but I didn't believe things ended well, like Mackenzie tried to spin it."

Mackenzie had kept the way he'd left under wraps? Sounded like something she would do. The woman was too tough for her own good. She needed to let people in. But then again she'd let him in, and he'd bailed on her.

"Over the years I kept thinking you'd contact her. Make things right."

"But I never did." He scraped his non-casted hand along the hair at the nape of his neck. "It wasn't like I didn't want to. I just didn't know what to say. How to say it."

Emma offered him an understanding smile. At least she didn't consider him a varmint. But then he hadn't left her high and dry. And Emma had always been homemade apple crisp with ice cream melting into the nooks and crannies, while Mackenzie was the kind of spicy dish that tore up your taste buds and still managed to leave a person wanting more.

If only a little of Emma's sugary demeanor would rub off on Mackenzie. Maybe then she'd actually hear him out. But Jace couldn't deny that the challenge of Mackenzie was exactly what had attracted him to her in the first place.

Which could turn out to be quite the problem this summer. Since he planned to go back to riding. Since he was an invalid, with all of these sidelining injuries. And since no matter what he did, Jace couldn't tame his attraction to the woman who wanted nothing to do with him. All because he refused to leave like she wanted him to… All because, the first time around, he'd left when she hadn't wanted him to.

But Kenzie Rae wasn't the only one who had issues and wants and demands. Jace had a few of his own. And if he didn't occupy himself with something useful this summer—like working at the ranch would provide for him—then he'd lose his mind even more than he already had when it had been demolished by the Widow Maker ride.

He'd worked hard this week to make himself useful, to stay busy, to help things run as smoothly as he could from his limited knowledge of the ranch. And Mackenzie refused to recognize that. All she could see was the trail of dust he'd left behind seven years ago.

Emma was studying the front office door Mackenzie had disappeared through, and Jace couldn't help wanting to ease the turmoil creasing her face. She wasn't in charge of fixing his and Mackenzie's past or current issues.

"I heard a rumor that the reason I haven't seen much of you is that you keep running off to spend time with your fiancé."

Just like that, her demeanor flipped and she turned all sparkling Emma, hands racing to cover pink cheeks. "It's true. I'm crazy about him. Can't seem to get enough. Thankfully, Mackenzie and Luc have been turning the other way when I keep sneaking off to meet him." Her lyrical laugh bubbled up. "That makes it sound so untoward. But it's not! I'm just..."

"Crazy in love."

"Exactly."

"I'm happy for you, Emma. If anyone deserves to be noticed and appreciated and cherished, it's you. Love looks good on you."

"Aw." She playfully shoved his arm. "You always were a sweet-talker." Her attention bounced over to Kenzie's wake again. "She's probably going to lose her mind if she comes back out here to find me consorting with the enemy." Her hand paused on his arm. "Be gentle with her, Jace. After you left..." She faltered and grew silent, her head shaking. "Did you know Luc left, too, shortly after you did?"

Oh. That wound opened up again. "I did not know that."

"He moved to Denver and came back eventually, but between the two of you, I wasn't sure what to do with Mackenzie."

Jace had so many questions. Like whether Emma thought Mackenzie would ever forgive him. Not to restart their relationship. He really couldn't do that when he planned to leave again. But he wouldn't mind getting along with the girl he'd once thought he'd marry.

"I really can't say more." Emma's hand squeezed his but dropped away. "Hang in there. If I know my sister, you're in for a fight if you plan to stick around."

Fight, he could do. And Mackenzie was worth it. Even if Jace was only here to right the wrong of their past. She deserved the truth from him—whenever she'd finally let him say it. His earlier doubts vanished. While his arm—and the rest of him—healed, he didn't have anywhere else to be.

Emma dropped into the chair across from Mackenzie's desk. The front office was surprisingly empty this afternoon, with everyone out with the guests, and Mackenzie had hoped to buckle down and get some work done—especially now that she didn't have Jace trailing her every move.

She'd only managed to train him Saturday, Sunday and Monday, and then she'd cut him loose. It wasn't enough. Of course, she should have done more for the sake of a well-run guest ranch.

But Mackenzie couldn't bring herself to continue.

She just kept hoping and praying that Jace would give up on his outrageous idea to work here for the summer and leave already. Preferably yesterday.

"How're you holding up?" Emma's question was soft and caring, but Mackenzie wasn't willing to go anywhere near the meaning behind it.

"Fine. Why wouldn't I be?"

Emma rolled her eyes. "Really? You might be able to get away with that attitude with the staff or a stranger, but I'm your sister. I know that Jace being here is killing you slowly."

"I can't… I just…don't want to talk about it. Him." Mackenzie didn't want to deal with the thought of Jace at all. That had been her plan for the week, and for the most part it was working.

Except she was exhausted.

Not being affected by Jace took all of her energy. Not letting the man crawl under her skin and set up camp was hard work. Not yelling at him for the way he'd left was, too.

Not caring about any of it like she'd hoped? Utterly impossible.

"You want me to beat him up for you?"

A laugh escaped. "Kinda, yeah. I'd like to see that."

"Hey, I can be tough when I need to be."

"I have no doubt about that, sister. So… what's going on with you?" Mackenzie motioned to Emma, desperate to change the subject. "I heard you come home late last night. I don't know how you're functioning on so little sleep, heading over to Gage's whenever you can."

"Nice conversation turn." Emma raised an eyebrow.

Mackenzie waited her out. Emma wouldn't push too much on Jace. She was too sympathetic and patient and understanding—qualities Mackenzie only possessed in small amounts.

"All right. I give. But I'm here if you need to talk to someone. Or vent. Okay?"

"Okay. Thanks." She might take Emma up on that offer if she had any idea how to deal with the jumbled, frustrating emotions Jace created in her.

"In answer to your question about me… I'm tired. I'm overwhelmed. I don't know how this summer is going to work. I miss Gage and Hudson so much already and this is only our first week. And on top of that, Hudson is sick."

Gratefulness at the turn in topic swelled, but then concern for Hudson took its place. "What kind of sick? Is he okay?" Emma's fiancé had become a guardian to the one-year-old boy recently, and Emma already loved the tyke as if he were her own.

"Nothing serious. At least I don't think so. Just a nasty cold. He's congested and has a runny nose. He's miserable and I didn't want to leave him or Gage to come home last night." A grin surfaced. "No offense."

"Ouch. You want to see your fiancé more than your sister? I'm wounded."

Humor tugged at the corner of her mouth. "It's just so hard not being there. Gage is doing his best, but he's drained. I am, too, from going back and forth. From trying to find a couple of minutes in the day or evening to sneak over there and see them. And then just when I get there it feels like I have to come home. And with Hudson sick, I'd like to be there to help. He was clinging to me last night." Her hands formed a self-hug, rubbing along the skin of her arms. "That's why I got home so late."

"So why don't you stay?"

"Ah, that's not really an option, as you know."

Mackenzie snorted. "Not like *that*. I

mean, are you ever going to change your mind about marrying Gage?"

Emma's head shook slowly. "No. Of course not."

"You don't have any doubts about him or Hudson." Mackenzie didn't say it like a question, because it wasn't. She already knew what Emma's response would be.

"No doubts about either of them. Of course not."

"So get married."

Confusion flickered. "We're planning to."

"I know you were thinking fall." Gage and Emma had tossed that idea around because both ranches slowed down and the schedule switched at Wilder Ranch. But that didn't mean they couldn't change their plans. They didn't have to follow some wedding protocol. "I'm saying get married sooner. What are you waiting for?"

Emma's mouth hung open wide enough that Mackenzie could toss a popcorn kernel into it without a problem—a game they'd played often as kids. One Mackenzie had always been the reigning champ of, much to Luc's frustration.

"Wait… What?"

"You want to be with Gage. That way you could be. After you're done with work, you'd go home and stay."

"Oh." Emma's eyes pooled with tears. "I want that."

"So get it. What do you really need to make a wedding happen?"

"Dress, pastor, flowers, food, people, place." Emma ticked items off on her fingers. "Mom and Dad. Gage's parents and his sister."

"You already have your dress picked out, right?"

She nodded, worrying her lip.

Of course, Emma had her dress picked out. The girl had probably been planning her wedding since she was five. Just like she probably had a Pinterest page filled with rustic, shabby-chic wedding ideas, like candles in mason jars and string lights, and the perfect shade of bridesmaid dresses. If anyone could pull a wedding together fast, it would be her.

"So, the biggest thing is family. And Pastor Higgin. Or you can always find another pastor to stand in if you need to—like the new assistant pastor at church."

"Actually…now that you mention it, Gage's parents are already coming at the end of July. I wonder if Mom and Dad could come, too. And his sister."

"That's a great idea. You could do a Saturday-evening wedding. The staff would rally to take care of things and complete the turnover for guests arriving Sunday. And you have so many friends you've helped over the years. You've been there for everyone. Let them be there for you. Mrs. Higgin could probably be convinced to make the cake. She's a fantastic baker. And you can ask for help with flowers and decorations. The only issue would be where."

She lit up. "I always imagined getting married here. Setting up chairs and a trellis in the grassy open space behind the lodge, with the mountains in the background. Casual and pretty."

"That makes it even easier if you don't have to find a venue."

"True." Emma bolted out of the chair and enveloped Mackenzie in a tight hug. "You're so right. This is the best idea you've ever had. Seriously, the best. Thank you, thank you, thank you." She let go and stood in a burst of energy. "I need to call Gage." And then she was off, with her phone in her hands. Mackenzie listened to the excited timbre of her voice for a few seconds before it faded away.

Emma had always been a bundle of cheerfulness. But Gage made her absolutely glow. Mackenzie didn't want to lose her sister, but she loved seeing her even happier than normal.

And really, shouldn't one of them be? Because ever since Jace had marched back into her world, Mackenzie wasn't confident she remembered how to get back to that feeling.

Probably wouldn't until he left again.

She'd been waiting all week for the man to hurry up and fail. For him to flounder. But he hadn't. So yeah, she'd thrown the square dancing at him as sabotage. If Jace couldn't figure it out, if he couldn't catch on, then he'd just have to leave.

And unlike the first time, that was exactly what Mackenzie wanted him to do.

Chapter Four

Mackenzie stood on a platform that towered above the forest floor. Gorgeous blue Colorado sky stretched above her. Bright green foliage spread out before her. It was a perfect day. Just the right temperature of warm but not too hot. Just the right everything.

She relaxed her legs and pushed off, her zip-line harness holding her as she flew through the path in the trees. Wind whipped by as she attempted to capture everything around her.

She reached the next tower and came to a stop, adjusting her T-shirt and shorts before taking off again. If only Luc and

Emma would consider her idea to build a zip-line course at Wilder Ranch. But Mackenzie would have to wait, because the next project they'd decided to undertake would be the ice-cream parlor and small store Emma had proposed. In the meantime she counted on a friend's offer to let her use their course whenever the desire struck.

And today she'd needed to soar.

She'd needed to escape Jace and everyone at the ranch.

And Luc had known it. Having someone attuned to your idiosyncrasies wasn't the worst thing in the world.

This morning he'd shown up at the door to the cabin she shared with Emma. "Why don't you get out of here for a bit today?" he'd said.

"But what about the turnover?"

"I can handle it. We'll survive without you. Take a break. For everyone's sake." He'd infused teasing into his tone, but fear had sent her body into a panicked sweat.

Had the whole world witnessed her agitation over the last week? Did everyone know how torn up she was about Jace working at Wilder Ranch?

"Is it that noticeable?"

"No," Luc had responded. "I just know you."

She'd almost burst into tears—proof that she was a hot mess in need of some Jace-free time in a Jace-free zone.

Thankfully Luc knew her well enough to rescue her from herself. When she'd tried to protest, to say that she'd stay so that he could spend time with Cate and Ruby, he'd simply hugged her. "I'm sorry I hired him without talking to you first."

And then he'd left before she could argue more.

Bless him. The offer—or command—had been a huge answer to her prayers. The past week had left Mackenzie frayed and on edge. With Jace invading every portion of her life—living in the guys' quarters at the ranch, present at every meal—she'd been unable to find her footing.

Mackenzie had heard enough "Jace is so

funny," "Jace is so great," "Jace did this" and "Jace did that" from both guests and staff that she wanted to cover her ears like a toddler.

He'd even come through with flying colors on the square dance last night. She'd arrived early, planning to save the evening and make sure the guests still had the experience they'd been promised, and there Jace had been—working out details and steps with the other staffers.

Things had gotten jumbled a few times during the night, but the guests hadn't cared. They'd loved every second. They'd loved Jace.

How come no one else saw through him to the man beneath that charming grin and those soulful chestnut eyes?

Mackenzie certainly did.

Clarification—she did now. In high school she hadn't. Back then she'd been intrigued by him. Jace probably still didn't know that she'd observed him for a few months before he'd talked to her. He'd been good at switching gears—one second sporting sad and serious, the next entertaining friends as the center of attention.

Once Mackenzie had gotten to know him, she'd realized it was his brother's accident that had broken him. Slowly but surely, as they'd hung out, Jace had shed that lost look. He'd bloomed back to life, and she'd fallen so hard for him.

No one had ever really gotten her the way Jace had.

They'd talked about getting married someday. Having kids. Where they'd live—somewhere near Westbend, because even back then Mackenzie hadn't wanted to leave Wilder Ranch. She'd somehow always known it was where she belonged.

She and Jace had been inseparable, and she'd had no reason to doubt him. That was why the fact that he'd left, and the way he'd done it, had been such a shock.

Why it had hurt so stinking bad.

What Jace had said to her in the lodge lobby yesterday had rattled around in her mind ever since. Was he right? Had he tried to tell her he wanted to continue competing at the next level after high school? She remembered maybe one instance like that and nothing more.

But maybe she hadn't been listening, like he'd claimed.

Still, if that were the case, he should have made his plans more clear. He should have made sure she understood.

And now the man should really stop expecting her to somehow get over his callous departure just because he'd decided to grace Wilder Ranch with his presence.

Last night, after the square dance, when she'd been trying to quietly escape, Jace had caught up to her in the hallway. He'd had the audacity to wink. And then he'd toggled his eyebrows and said, "One word. YouTube."

YouTube. That was how he'd figured out the dance? The man had to be kidding. Except he wasn't.

A crease had split his forehead. "You're

irritated that I handled tonight well, aren't you? Still don't want me here, do you?"

"Nope." The truth had just skipped right out.

"You could take a minute. Think about your answer. Give the illusion of grace."

"Nope." Mackenzie had wanted nothing more than to flee, but then Jace had wrenched the conversation up another level, while his voice had dipped low and meaningful.

"You ever going to forgive me for leaving the way I did?"

She hadn't spoken. There'd been no need to repeat the word that still fitted a third time.

Jace's fist had clenched, and his lips had pressed tight. And then he'd turned back to the guests, to the staff, to what was supposed to be her world. He'd left her standing there, wrestling a supersize hissy fit into submission.

Composure was usually her thing. Nothing ruffled Mackenzie unless she let it.

But Jace Hawke broke all of her rules.

Mackenzie finished the rest of the zip-line course quickly. The temptation to fly through it a third time was herculean strong, but she couldn't.

She should really get back to the ranch and make sure everything was going smoothly with the turnover for the guests that would arrive tomorrow. Mackenzie had fitted in a hike before zip-lining, so she'd already been gone for hours.

She probably shouldn't have left in the first place, but Luc had been right—she'd needed it. Time away from the ranch—from Jace—had been good for her. She already felt lighter, better.

The drive back went way too fast.

When she turned down the ranch drive, agitation rose up and choked her. Mackenzie loved this place. Always had. But Jace was ruining that for her, too.

Was she crazy to be this upset with him for sticking around? With the way he'd left… How much he'd hurt her… Nope. She had a right to be mad. But holding on to that anger was draining her.

Mackenzie parked at the lodge, planning to head inside, check on how things were going. But before she could even open the door of her little pickup truck, Jace stood next to it.

She ignored him and took her time switching from her tennis shoes over to flip-flops, then tossed the hiking shoes to the passenger floor of her truck.

Jace must have swallowed one of her impatient pills, because he hauled open her driver's door.

"What do you want, Hawke?" Why did he have to be the first person she saw when she returned? Hadn't God heard her prayers this week? She'd been requesting less Jace, not more, but the opposite kept happening.

Concern radiated from him, tightening his features. "You have your phone with you today?"

"Yes, but it's on Silent." Otherwise it would have been going off the whole time. Mackenzie had known Luc would handle things, so she'd gone off the radar. "I forgot to check it when I got back into my truck."

She winced. That hadn't been smart of her. "Why? Is something wrong with the turnover?"

"No." Jace rubbed a hand over the slight stubble on his cheeks and chin. His eyes—they stayed tender. Sympathetic. Something *was* wrong.

"What is it? What's going on?"

"It's Cate. She went into early labor. She and Luc are in Denver."

"Wait, what? But isn't it too early? Are they trying to stop the labor?"

"She was too far along to stop it. Luc just talked to Emma. Cate had the babies."

"Already?" How was that possible? Mackenzie had only been gone for a handful of hours.

"The girls are tiny but getting good care. But Cate…"

Dread wrapped talons around her windpipe. "But Cate what?"

"She's having complications. She's losing blood. Luc didn't tell Emma much. He had to go. He just said to pray."

Oh, God. I take it all back. How could I complain about such trivial matters like Jace being back in my life? I promise I'll be better. I'll be more mature. Please don't let anything happen to Cate or the babies. Luc would never recover. None of us would.

Mackenzie stared out the front windshield of her truck. "This can't be happening. Everything was fine when I left this morning." How could the world just tip upside down like that?

"Since the staff knows about Cate, Emma took Ruby over to Gage's to prevent her from hearing anyone talk about… any of it. No need to scare the girl. Then she'll take Ruby to see Cate and the girls if…*when* Luc gives the okay."

"That's good." *Breathe, Mackenzie. Breathe.* "Emma's the best with her."

"Ruby would have been good with you, too. You just weren't here as an option."

Mackenzie was certain Jace hadn't meant that comment the way she'd taken it. But it was still true. Her brother had needed her. There'd been an emergency, and she hadn't been here, because she'd been too busy being immature and running away. Sure, Luc had told her to, but she shouldn't have listened. She should have handled being around Jace better, so that hiding wouldn't have been necessary. She should have stopped throwing toddler tantrums and done her job.

"I need to go. I need to be there." *I need to see my brother, to know he's okay. And in order for him to be okay, Cate needs to be okay. Okay, God? Please.* But how could Mackenzie leave the ranch with no one in charge? "But I can't leave the staff with the turnover. If Luc's not here, Emma either—"

"It's taken care of," Jace interrupted.

"How? You've never even been here for it before."

"Your staff, although new, has been well trained, and you have lists written up for everything. We knocked most of it out, and they know what else is left to do. They wanted to help. This is all they've got right now, and they're on it."

Sounded like Jace had been on it, too. Guilt rose up. They'd needed him already. Luc had been right to hire Jace without her consent, for the sake of the ranch. And if things were taken care of, that gave Mackenzie permission to go see her brother. And Cate. Because she was trusting that Cate would be all right. She was clinging to that.

"My keys." She checked the ignition. Not there. Where had she put them?

"I'll drive you." Jace held her keys in the palm of his hand.

What? How and when had he snagged them?

Maybe she'd dropped them when she'd first arrived. Who knew? Who cared?

"I'm fine, thanks. I can drive myself."

Jace's fist closed around the metal. "You're a mess right now. I'm not letting you drive."

Puh-lease. She wasn't some baby who needed to be coddled. "I'm fine. Give me my keys." The demand came out clipped and desperate. "I need to get going."

"No." Jace's arms crossed. "I can drive you or we can stand here and waste more time fighting. Can you just trust me on this? You're shaking right now."

"I am *not*." She held out her hand to prove it, and it vibrated before her like a cup of coffee on the dash of a car. *Great*. How nice of her body to betray her.

"You're not driving my truck."

"Okay. I'll drive mine." The man strode across the gravel, to his vehicle. "Come on, Wilder, you're wasting time."

He had her keys. She wanted to scream and kick and throw a fit, but he was right. It would just waste time. If Mackenzie wanted to see her brother right now, which she did, she didn't have a choice.

Jace had never seen Mackenzie so shaken. And rightfully so. The news from Luc had been sporadic. Only that the babies were small and early. And that Cate had lost a lot of blood—had still been losing blood when Luc had talked to Emma. He'd said that the doctors were trying to stop the hemorrhaging, and that was all of the information they had.

Jace didn't know how to help or comfort. So he'd settled for getting Mackenzie safely to where she wanted to be.

They'd been in his truck for ten minutes, and the woman had yet to make a peep. He'd asked her to let Emma know they were headed to Denver. She'd texted, then let her phone fall to the truck bench seat. Since then she'd been staring out the window, like her whole world had crashed down around her. And it had. Mackenzie was incredibly close to her brother. Her twin. She was likely kicking herself for not being there today, when Cate had gone into labor and things had progressed so quickly.

Maybe he could get her talking, get her to focus on something else.

"Where'd you run off to today?"

Her wince was quick but noticeable. "Luc told me to take some time off, so I did. I hiked and then zip-lined. A friend owns a course, and he lets me go for free whenever."

He. Was this *he* young or old? "Boyfriend of yours or something?"

She snorted. "He's nineteen. Actually, his parents own it, but he runs it most of the time."

"And gives out free passes to gorgeous women."

Her face pinked, accompanied by an eye roll and a shake of her low ponytail. "No. That's not how it is."

She was getting riled now, but at least some color was rushing back to her skin and her breathing wasn't so shallow.

"I mean, he's asked me out before, but he's too young for me. I've told him countless times."

Jace narrowly avoided sprouting a smile. Young pup was probably smitten with Mackenzie. He didn't blame the kid.

"Do you normally take off on Saturdays?"

"No. After the staff is well trained, I

could. I don't technically need to be there if they can handle things."

"But you usually are."

"Why not? Luc tries to spend time with Cate and Ruby after the guests leave. I don't have anywhere else to be, so I make sure things run smoothly. I should have been there today, especially with all of our new staff. But I just..." Her vision tracked out the window again, and she didn't finish her statement. Didn't elaborate.

"It's me, isn't it? You were escaping from me." Luc had told him that Mackenzie had taken part of the day off, that she'd needed to blow off some steam.

More like blow off some Jace.

A huff of air filled the cab. "Let's just let it go, okay? It doesn't matter. I wasn't where I was supposed to be, and now my brother's wife is having serious complications."

"That has nothing to do with you and where you were, Kenzie Rae, and you know it."

"I know nothing of the sort. What if I could have helped? What if—"

"Stop it." Jace softened his command by giving her arm a quick squeeze. His thumb etched across her skin before he let go and moved it back to the steering wheel, to keep from driving with his casted arm. "You couldn't have changed a thing. They left quickly. He didn't wait for you, if that's what you're worried about."

A hurt-animal noise tore from her throat. This woman.

"I didn't mean it like that. Just meant that he didn't waste any time. You don't get to blame yourself." Was that what had Kenzie so upset? That she wasn't needed? That Luc had left without her being there?

"Emma… She told me Luc left not too long after I did."

Jace watched the car in front of him change lanes as Mackenzie studied him. At least the concussion hadn't stolen his peripheral vision from him.

"He did." Her body gave a telltale tremor. Like a secret admission she would never give away herself. Jace hated that he'd hurt her. That had never been his intent. And yes, he wished he would have handled things differently after high school. But the truth was, he'd been so in love with the woman across the seat of the truck from him, he would never have been able to walk away from her if he'd said goodbye.

The hold would have been too strong.

And Mackenzie was built for Wilder Ranch. He couldn't picture her anywhere else. It fitted her the way riding did him.

They were made for two different worlds, and a hefty chunk of time hadn't changed that.

"Feels just like when we were kids." Mackenzie spoke quietly, then rubbed her arms like she was chilled. The reaction had to be emotional, because his truck was toasty with the sun cascading in the windows.

"What do you mean?"

He didn't expect an answer from her. Kenzie wasn't in the business of telling him anything lately. But today's trauma must have messed with her tongue, because she kept going.

"When Luc had open-heart surgery, they forgot about me."

His gut clenched. "Who did?"

"Mom and Dad. They had to be up and out of the house early, and my aunt was staying with us, but I'd said I wanted to see him in the morning. Before they left. I don't know if they didn't believe me or what, but I woke up and they were gone. Luc was gone." Her sadness swelled and filled the cab of the truck. "I was so haunted by the thought that I might never see him again or that he might not make it through the surgery. I was a mess that whole day, until we heard the surgery went well."

Jace pictured her at that young age. Left. Alone. Missing her twin. She and Luc had always been close. Connected.

For him to be gone without her getting to say goodbye—for her to wonder about his well-being during open-heart surgery. Ouch. That was a lot for a kid to bear.

It hurt just hearing her talk about it. And for her to still be holding on to that this many years later…that moment, that pain, must have remained all of this time.

Jace couldn't believe she was telling him this. He wanted to reach out and touch her again. To ground himself and her. But there wasn't anything he could do to stop the flow of blood from that particular wound.

Because when he'd left town, he'd only added to it. And then Luc right after him.

Turns out the most un-leave-able person Jace knew had been left on repeat.

Chapter Five

Jace transported them to the hospital as fast as his truck and traffic would allow. They didn't receive any updates on the way, and he was afraid to ask. If there were good news, Luc would have contacted them.

Mackenzie must have felt the same, because unease and fear radiated from her, sending currents bouncing off the metal framework of the cab.

"Have you heard from Emma?"

Mackenzie picked up her phone. "No. I'll ask if she knows anything new." Her thumbs flew over the keys. Her phone chimed almost immediately. "She hasn't heard from him either." She dropped the phone into her lap. "Do you still believe in God?"

Why would she ask him something like that? The woman kept assuming he'd changed with time, but he hadn't. And no one knew him like she did. Not his mom. Not his brother. Not even his rodeo buddies.

"Of course I do." Kenzie could question all she wanted, but Jace was still the same. He'd even prayed for her through all of these years. For her happiness, her success. That someday she'd be able to understand why he'd done things the way he had. That someday she'd forgive him for it. "I've been praying nonstop about Cate and the girls, if that's what you're asking."

Again with that study of him from the side. Jace let it slide, let her look, thinking maybe she'd finally see him for who he really was. Who he'd always been, minus the blip of leaving her after high school.

"Me, too." She found a piece of thread on the bottom of her shirt and twisted it round and round her finger. Mackenzie normally wore jeans and boots at the ranch, but today she was casual in a bright blue T-shirt, shorts and flip-flops. Her feet and legs were tanned, her toenails unpainted. She was the kind of pretty that couldn't come from a jar or a tube. It simply was.

"Emma said they called the church prayer chain. The whole town of Westbend is probably on their knees."

"Then let's believe God is listening."

Jace parked in the hospital lot. He hopped out and then waited by the front of the truck for Mackenzie, not about to open her door or help her in any way. He wasn't that daring.

She met him near the still-heated engine. "You don't need to come in, you know." Her stormy eyes landed everywhere but on him. "I'm fine. You can head back home if you want." She motioned as if he were a fly she could shoo away. "Or go do something else...fun, in Denver. I'll get a ride back."

Fun? Was she nuts? Like he would go

anywhere else right now. Mackenzie might not want his support, but it was hers anyway.

"Stop it. Please." He placed his hands—the left bulky with the cast—on her shoulders. It was the closest they'd been since his arrival at the ranch, but Jace no longer cared about whatever barriers Mackenzie had built. Those pretty grays, crammed with upset and worry, finally met his and held. "What happened between us in the past doesn't matter right now. This is bigger than that." She didn't move away, didn't disconnect from him.

"Okay." Her shoulders eased down under his grip, her chin jutting in agreement.

She'd given him an inch, and Jace wanted ten miles. The craving to haul her close and hold on was almost impossible to resist.

But he managed to. She was letting him in the slightest bit, and he refused to ruin that.

They walked toward the entrance, Kenzie's strides sure and strong. But that didn't hide the fact that whatever they were about to face inside the hospital walls was scaring her silly.

Him, too.

The woman behind the information desk directed them. When they reached the correct floor and stepped out of the elevator, Kenzie gave a quiet gasp as the door slid shut behind them. Luc was sitting on the floor outside a room about halfway down a long florescent-lit hallway. His knees were bent, his head crashed onto his arms.

It didn't look good.

For the whole drive Jace had been telling himself that when they got to the hospital, everything would be okay. That the news would be encouraging. That maybe Luc hadn't contacted Emma or Mackenzie because he'd been busy with Cate or the babies.

But now? Jace's theory was in question. Big time.

Helplessness suffocated him. He was worthless here. He didn't have the right to comfort Mackenzie anymore. Not like she would need if things had worsened.

She might not want him in her life, but he could be strong for her.

Jace could at least do that.

He'd failed her in the past. Maybe he could figure out how to make that up to her now and in the future.

Mackenzie's overcooked-noodle knees buckled at the sight of her strong brother crashed to the floor in the hospital hallway. With his head dropped to his arms, he didn't see them. Didn't know she'd faltered so hard that Jace had cupped her elbow and now held her steady.

She wanted to shake Jace off, but she was frozen and immovable. A mess. Mackenzie had never felt so helpless and woozy and worthless, and it was embarrassing. *Enough. This moment isn't about you. Go be there for your brother.* But what if things were worse? What if Cate...?

A boulder clogged Mackenzie's throat,

making it impossible to swallow, to suck in oxygen. Numbness buzzed through her limbs.

"Breathe." Jace jiggled her arm. "In and out."

She obeyed like a weak, pitiful kitten who needed to be bottle-fed.

Her brother was in a heap, and she was so cemented and freaked out that she couldn't make her legs work in order to go to him. She was supposed to be the strong one. But the crown no longer fitted.

"You don't know what's going on. Don't jump to conclusions." Jace nodded toward Luc, his voice quiet and annoyingly calm. "Go find out, and then you can deal with it, whatever it is. You can handle this. You're the strongest person I know." Mackenzie wanted to be mad at Jace for driving her here. For forcing her to ride with him. For not leaving her alone.

But she was pathetically grateful he hadn't let her get away with any of that.

The temptation to turn into him for just a second, to let those strong arms of his tighten around her and that familiar voice whisper in her ear that everything was going to be okay, even if it wasn't… Mackenzie wanted that like she'd never wanted anything before.

And she hated herself for that weakness.

You've been just fine without him for seven years. Jace Hawke does not need to carry you through this. You have God and your family, and they're enough. Those sources are trustworthy, and the man next to you is not.

Not anymore.

"I'm going to find a waiting room and some bad coffee. I have no doubt you'd rather me not be with you right now, and I get that. So go check in with your brother. I'll keep praying."

Stop it! Stop being so good to me.

It wasn't fair. Jace's support only reminded her of what could have been. If he hadn't left Westbend. If he hadn't left her.

She didn't want to give him the satisfaction of seeing her unravel, so Mackenzie filled her lungs and pushed her shoulders back.

Jace watched her, assessing. Probably

checking to see if she was going to fall apart right in front of him. Again.

"I'm fine, Hawke."

"You're going to have to trademark that phrase pretty soon, Kenzie Rae."

"Don't *Kenzie Rae* me."

"But it's so much fun to make you mad. How can I resist?"

The faintest hint of normalcy, of humor, edged in with his teasing. But the heavy unknown future loomed bigger, and they both knew it.

"Thanks." That was all she said, all she could muster. Jace accepted it with a nod, then walked in the opposite direction.

He's not the worst guy in the world.

And that was exactly the problem. He'd been the best guy in her world once upon a time, and she hadn't wanted that to change.

But sometimes Mackenzie didn't get to make the decisions. They were made for her.

She could only pray this wasn't one of those moments and that what she was about to find out from her brother would be the good news she and Jace and countless others had been praying for.

Even though her brother's body language shouted the opposite of that.

It took Mackenzie ages to cross the speckled, bleached tiles.

When she finally made it to her brother, she didn't speak. She was so afraid to ask what was wrong and find out the answer was horrible that she just dropped to the floor next to him and mirrored his bent-knee position.

His head came up from his hands. His eyes were wet. Red-lined. The only memory Mackenzie had of Luc getting emotional was on his wedding day. When Cate and Ruby had come down the aisle together—then his Adam's apple had bobbed, and he'd had to work to keep himself in check.

But that was about it.

"How is she?"

"She's okay." Luc rubbed his hands over his face as if trying to wipe clean a chalkboard. "She's okay now. She made a turn for the better. Finally. They thought they were going to have to do a hysterectomy. But at the last second the bleeding stopped." He choked back a sob. "The nurses are in there now, helping her, and I was in the way, so I came out here to pull myself together."

Mackenzie grabbed him and held on.

A half groan, half cry wrenched from Luc, near her ear. "What would I have done…? What if she hadn't…?" His anguish was palpable, registering in her bones.

"It's okay. It's okay. She's all right now." *Thank You, thank You, thank You, God.*

Mackenzie didn't know what else to say or do to comfort Luc, so she just hugged him and prayed silently, praising God that Cate and Luc's story got to be one of the good ones.

They released each other, and Luc inhaled, deep and relieved. His mouth opened and then closed as if he couldn't form words.

"You don't have to say anything else. I

get it." Luc might not be able to express himself at the moment, but Mackenzie could read him loud and clear. She'd always known what Luc was thinking or feeling. It had been unnerving at times to be so connected to another human being. But then it had also felt completely normal, because she'd never known anything else.

They sat silently for a minute, Luc stitching himself together, Mackenzie giving him the space to do that.

"You have to see the girls." He lit up, dissolving the stark pain from only moments before. "They look so identical, I'm worried I'm not going to be able to tell them apart. And they're so tiny and perfect that I'm afraid I'm going to break them if I pick them up. Not that I've had much of a chance to do that yet. They're in the NICU now."

"I can't wait to see them. Are you finally going to reveal their names? It was incredibly annoying that you didn't tell us before they were born."

Her brother obviously found her impatience amusing, because he waited a few beats before finally spilling. "Everly Jane and Savannah Rae."

"You used our middle names? Emma's going to flip. Oh, I love the names. So sweet. I'm honored."

"The babies will be here for a while, gaining weight and developing their lungs, but it sounds like they're doing well, considering."

"Emma's going to kill me for getting to them first. She took Ruby over to Gage's. Since everyone at the ranch knew about Cate, they didn't want her to overhear anything. She's waiting for the all clear to bring Ruby to see the babies and you guys."

"That was a good idea. I need to call her and let her know Cate's through the worst of it."

"I will."

"That would be great. Thanks. So, how did you even know what happened? I tried to call you earlier today, but your phone must have been off."

"It was on Silent. I'm so sorry. I wish I could have been there for you guys." It might take Mackenzie a few weeks or months to stop kicking herself for being gone during an emergency. Jace's statement in the car that her presence wouldn't have changed anything might be logical, but she still didn't like that she'd gone off the grid. Or that she'd let Jace affect her so much that avoiding him had been the immature reason she'd needed to escape at all. "Jace told me when I got back to the ranch. And then he insisted on driving me here. I guess he thought I was too upset to drive. I don't know what that was about. I was fine." *Or I would have been. Somehow.*

"Ah, Kenzie. You're a stubborn piece of work—you know that?"

"You mean I'm fabulous? Irreplaceable? A true superwoman?"

Luc groaned and stood, then tugged her up. "Right. All of those things." She even earned a quarter smile. "Maybe you shouldn't be so hard on him."

She wrinkled her nose.

"I have a favor to ask of you."

A switch in subject matter? Yes, please. "Of course. Whatever you need. Coffee? Food? Clothes?"

"I'm sure it will come as no surprise that our bags were packed by Cate, and we have every possible item we might need, here with us. Except car seats. But we won't be needing those for a while."

Mackenzie grinned. "I should have seen that one coming." Cate was nothing if not organized. "So, what is it?"

"I get that I ruined your life by hiring Jace without talking to you first." Oh, boy. So, they were continuing down the Jace road. "And I love you enough that if I could change that and find someone else, I would in a heartbeat."

Her own heart bogged down like a boot stuck in mud. Luc wouldn't have hired Jace if she'd just been honest about how things had ended between them. How much he'd hurt her. It was more her fault than anyone's that the man was working at Wilder Ranch.

"But I can't," Luc continued. "He's all we have right now. And I need to be here for Cate and the girls. We're probably going to be driving back and forth between the ranch and Denver plenty. I'm not sure when the girls will get to go home. Cate either. I need you to buck up for the summer and accept Jace's help. Train him."

"I did."

That look he gave her. It was *I know you better than that* and *you're digging a hole* all in one. "I mean train him all the way this time. And quit trying to get him to leave."

"But—"

"Do you really think I don't know what you've been up to?"

Well. "This is all making me feel like a huge idiot." She huffed, humiliation and regret wrapped up together. It was like when she'd been a kid and thought she was getting away with something only to find out that her parents had been onto her the whole time.

And she'd definitely been childlike about Jace.

"I'm sorry I've been a big ole baby. I get it. And you're right. I'll stop. Promise. You don't need to worry about a thing with the ranch. We'll handle it. I'll even force myself into your office to make sure people and bills are paid and the lights stay on. Don't worry about a thing. Seriously. I've got it covered." She swallowed the bitter truth of her next statement. "I mean, Jace and I have it covered."

"Good. Thank you." Luc nodded just as the nurses came out of Cate's room. "I'm going in to see my wife. You coming?"

"In a minute." She wanted to give Luc and Cate some time together without her intrusion. Plus she needed a second to deal with the mortification she was currently drowning in.

Luc strode into the room, shutting the door behind him, and Mackenzie barely resisted banging her head against the wood.

How embarrassing! She'd been a scheming toddler about Jace, and the whole world knew it. Well, maybe not the whole world. But her brother was bad enough.

Why had she been so immature about the man? They were long over and done. There was no need to stay tangled up in the past. In a should-have-meant-nothing high school relationship.

Mackenzie hated admitting she'd been wrong in how she'd been acting. And it was like chewing sand to think about being civil to Jace, to think about welcoming him and not just tolerating the guy who'd once made her feel so trivial that she hadn't even been worthy of a goodbye.

But for her brother's sake—for the ranch's sake—she would do exactly that.

If she were truly over Jace, there would be no harm in letting him back into her life. Professionally speaking, of course.

Chapter Six

Jace had been summoned by his *boss*, Mackenzie, and he wasn't about to be late.

The two of them had been running, heads down, since the babies' arrival nine days ago. After Cate's discharge from the hospital, she and Luc had stayed in Denver for a few days, to be close to the girls, who still needed to reach some milestones before they'd be allowed to come home. Now Luc and Cate were spending nights at the ranch and driving to the hospital during the day.

Thankfully Mama Wilder had come to help watch Ruby for a few days, because Jace didn't know how Mackenzie and Emma would have added that to their full plates.

He'd jumped in with both boots since the twins' unexpected early arrival, trying to be a help, hoping that his being here somehow made it easier for Luc to be there for his wife and daughters.

At least that would lessen the sting of not being able to compete. A couple of Jace's buddies had texted him about what he'd missed, updating him, asking how he was. Jace hadn't responded yet. If he didn't soon, they'd come knocking on his door. But it was hard to be out of the loop, not earning points. At least the guys would understand that.

Jace had just gotten back from supervising the afternoon shooting-range session, and Kenzie had said to meet him by the corral, but she wasn't there when he arrived.

Sable, the buckskin quarter horse who'd caught his attention last week, approached, meeting him at the railing.

"Hey there, pretty girl." She whinnied,

then nosed around, looking for a treat. "You think that I'm going to bring you something every time I say hi?"

Her head bobbed in answer, and he laughed. "Fine. I give." Jace had popped into the kitchen on his way over and snagged an apple for Sable.

He offered it to her, and she chomped the treat. After, she nuzzled his shirt and his shoulders. "You're not nearly as stingy with your affection as some women I know." One woman in particular. Not that Jace was trying to win Mackenzie's affection.

But even though they'd worked together all week and done a good job of it—at least according to him—there was still a line in the sand. One Mackenzie had drawn and didn't dare cross. There'd been no talk about anything personal. Just business. It made sense, but at some point the two of them were going to have to stop pretending they didn't have a past.

"I guess the timing's not right yet. I can be patient."

With Luc's absence, there hadn't really been an opportunity to discuss anything outside Wilder Ranch.

It had been trial-by-fire learning for Jace, because while Mackenzie had attempted to train him more in the last week, their time was often cut short or interrupted.

But it was working. Jace was figuring things out. So he had no idea why Mackenzie had called this impromptu meeting with him.

Maybe she still wanted him to leave, though she hadn't given him that impression since the hospital. Mackenzie had been on her best behavior. He wasn't sure whether to be grateful for that or concerned about what she wasn't saying.

Jace brushed his free hand down Sable's neck, her coat gleaming in the sunlight. "You could rub off on her, you know. You're as sweet as they come." She held his gaze, those deep, dark eyes seeing and understanding more than anyone probably gave them credit for. "You're right. That wouldn't be nearly as interesting, would it? I always did like that Kenzie Rae was made of spice." Sable pawed the ground. "You have some sass in you, too, girl. No need to get in a huff about it."

That seemed to placate the horse, who burrowed her nose into his shirt in search of another treat. "I gave you all I've got. And don't tell the other horses that I'm sneaking you contraband. Pretty sure the *boss* would be upset about that." Jace's cheeks crinkled at the picture of Kenzie taking him to task. Her spunk was exactly what attracted him to her. Kenzie Rae could rule the world with one glance. When Jace had first noticed her in high school, it hadn't taken him long to "happen" to walk by her locker just as they were both headed to shop class—as if her signing up for shop class hadn't been enough of a reason to fall in love with her right then and there. And it hadn't taken her long to challenge him to a competition at the Wilder Ranch's shooting range.

The first day they'd hung out had stretched, morphing from shooting to riding the ranch and then dinner with the Wilder family.

Jace had fallen for all of it—her, her family, her world.

They'd quickly become inseparable.

Maybe they'd moved too quickly into a relationship for their young ages. But it hadn't felt like it. It had felt like he'd found the one for him and age didn't matter one hoot.

And kissing the woman? It was like watching a fireworks show from five feet away and somehow managing not to get burned. "She can kiss. I'll give her that." Those lips held just as much spark as the rest of her. There might be one thousand off-limits signs between him and Mackenzie, but Jace wouldn't mind a quick refresher in that area. "Not that she wants a kiss from me these days. So I guess we don't have to worry about that, do we, Sable-girl?"

"You're not slipping the horses treats now, are you, Hawke?" Mackenzie startled him, and Jace jumped like he was guilty.

Since he'd been thinking about kissing his boss, he supposed he sort of was.

"Of course not." He turned and flashed an innocent grin. Mackenzie was about ten feet away and still approaching. Had she heard his earlier comments? Should he ask…or no? A glint registered in those storm-cloud eyes for just a second before it was gone.

Even in her Wilder Ranch gear—polo, jeans and boots—Mackenzie was the picture of summer. Her wavy hair shifted in the breeze, and Jace's mouth turned to sand at the sight of her. He was once again the high school version of himself, smitten with the girl who'd breathed life into him after Evan's accident.

"I see you're playing favorites." Mackenzie's nod encompassed Sable, and Jace barely resisted snorting at where his mind had gone instead. He'd really never had another favorite—or another girlfriend—besides Mackenzie.

"Well, she's hard to resist." If Mackenzie had any inkling he was referring to her, she didn't let on.

"Sorry I'm late. Mom's here, as you know, and Emma had to talk to us. She'd decided that with the added stress of the twins still in the hospital, Luc and Cate going back and forth all of the time, and the strain that creates on the rest of us, she and Gage should postpone the wedding or just get married at the courthouse instead of having it here, at the end of July like they'd planned."

"Sounds like Emma."

"Doesn't it? Mom talked her off the ledge. She reminded her that they're planning to have a simple ceremony and reception, and that everything would calm down soon and work out like it's supposed to. And that Luc and Cate would be incredibly upset if she changed her wedding because of them or the girls."

"Sounds like Mama Wilder handled everything just fine."

"Oh, man." Mackenzie's head shook. "I haven't heard that name in so long. I forgot you used to call her that."

He sure had. He'd practically been a Wilder family member those last couple of years. Another reason it had been so hard for him to leave. He hadn't just torn himself away from Mackenzie; he'd ripped his heart out by leaving all of them.

"So, what's up? Did you ask to meet me out here so you could fire me? Or kill me and hide the body?"

Her eyes crinkled at the corners, and her level of pretty about knocked him over. "No." Her head tilted. "Though you are giving me ideas."

"Very funny."

"Honestly? I was desperate to get outside. I hate being in the office on a gorgeous day like this."

Jace couldn't agree more. "Luc's work driving you crazy?"

She waved a hand. "Nah. It's been all right."

He raised questioning eyebrows and waited.

A reluctant shrug followed. "Okay, so it's not my favorite. But after everything that happened with Cate and the babies, the last thing I'm going to do is complain. And in regard to your earlier remark, I'm pretty certain I've been on my best behavior around you. I haven't said one unkind thing to you in the last week."

"You been keeping track?"

"Maybe. Maybe I'm rather proud of myself."

This woman. "You're a piece of work—you know that?"

"I've heard that before, yes." A smile. An actual full-fledged smile followed, along with a jolt of attraction from him. *She's your boss, not your girlfriend. Cool it, Hawke.*

"Luc said that you could teach the wranglers some things, even if you can't do them yourself because of your arm. Is that true?"

She was asking what he could add to the ranch, not pressuring him to leave yet again? Jace willed his jaw not to fall open in shock.

"Sure. We could do steer wrestling. Cattle roping. Not sure exactly how to teach those with the arm, but I'd figure it out." Jace glanced at the intrusive cast. He'd been taking every supplement he could find that promoted faster healing. And something must be working, because when he'd checked in with Dr. Sanderson this week, he'd shown improvement in all areas.

Even his noggin had calmed down over the last few days, giving him hope his symptoms were finally subsiding.

"I should be able to talk some of the guys through it. Not like they'd be competing in a real rodeo. Just against each other."

"As long as it's something the wranglers can do without getting hurt, I think the guests would love it."

"As for team penning..." Jace scanned the corral. "I'm not sure we can swing it. Usually it's culling certain cattle from a herd. So we'd need livestock for that. But we could do a makeshift version where the wranglers just have to corral three cattle. Something simple like that. It would probably still be entertaining for the guests.

We could have them compete against each other for fastest times."

"That would work."

"Does this conversation mean you're accepting that Luc hired me and you're going to stop trying to get rid of me?"

A dash of *don't push me too far* mingled with a faint smile. "Seems like it."

"Does this also mean we're going to get along now instead of all of that angry sassiness and chilly ignoring me?"

Her thumb traced the scar on her arm that had come from attempting to sneak through a barbed-wire fence as a kid. "I haven't done that in forever." She paused. "At least not for over a week."

"True." A weak and yet somehow amusing defense.

"And my answer is maybe. If you'll do one thing for me."

Warning sirens blared. "And what's that?"

"Teach me to ride a bull."

"What?" No way, no how would Jace put

the woman he'd once loved up on one of those bucking beasts. "You're joking, right?"

"Nope. I don't see why the boys get to have all the fun."

"That's what will help you get along with me?"

She huffed. "Luc already commanded me to do that. But let's just say the bull riding lesson might bring to life my more… generous, patient, forgiving side."

Jace hadn't known she had one of those. Only Kenzie Rae. And despite understanding the appeal of riding a bull, he couldn't do it. He'd never forgive himself if she got hurt. And she would. Everyone did eventually.

"I'll teach you something else. What about cattle roping?"

"No. I want the real deal."

"Ah, no. That's way too dangerous."

"You do it."

"I'm a man."

Fire lit her features, and Jace threw his head back and laughed deep and long. "I'm kidding." He tried to catch his breath, slapping a hand against his sternum. "I'm joking." His arms formed a protective barrier in case she attacked him for the chauvinistic reply. Of course he hadn't meant it in the least. He'd just wanted to get a rise out of Mackenzie. "I knew your reaction to that would be hilarious."

"Har-har." She was all annoyance, but he was positive her lips held the slightest curve.

"Kenzie Rae, I have no doubt you can do anything you put your mind to, and that being female doesn't change what you can accomplish, but I'm not teaching you to ride a bull. I can't. It's too dangerous and I'd never forgive myself if you got hurt."

"You're hurt right now!" She motioned toward his arm.

"Exactly my point."

A strangled *argh* came from her. "Fine. I'll find someone else to help me."

"No, you won't. You certainly wouldn't be asking me if you had any other options."

That punch-him-in-the-gut mouth angled up at the corners. "True."

"You already said we were going to get along now. You can't take that back just because I refuse to get you injured on a bull."

"Don't tell me what I can and can't do, Hawke."

He groaned. She laughed—actually laughed. The sound was painful and delicious all at the same time.

"Come on." Mackenzie strode toward the barn. "Let's go see what supplies we have and what we'll need to get."

Jace jogged after her, and out of nowhere his head spun and reeled.

Seriously? He'd barely moved at all. How could something so simple cause such a reaction? Frustration choked him. Just when he'd thought the dizziness and headaches had packed up and left for good, the symptoms reared up again.

He hadn't even put medicine in his pocket, because the last couple of days had been great.

He slowed to hopefully combat the vertigo, and Mackenzie paused to wait for him, confusion at his snail pace puckering her brow. "You okay?"

"Yep." Nope. Not in the least.

Jace might have just made the slightest hint of progress with Mackenzie, but the rest of him was still barreling downhill.

Jace walked with Mackenzie as they entered the barn, but something about the last few seconds niggled and latched on. What had that been about? It had almost looked like Jace had swayed after he'd jogged in her direction.

But that was impossible. The man rode bulls for a living. He jumped to safety when his eight seconds were up—or got thrown before that, if the bull bested him. So the idea of him wobbling after a few steps didn't make sense at all.

Maybe she'd imagined it.

Except...that wasn't the first time Mackenzie had noticed him acting strange. There'd been the day they'd ridden the trails and he'd claimed he was overheated, out by the hot springs. And the day the twins were born…on the way out of the hospital, that night, Jace had tossed her his truck keys and told her to drive. Mackenzie had assumed he'd been offering her an olive branch—making up for his churlish behavior earlier in the day, when he'd insisted on driving her to the hospital. But then on the ride home, he'd let his head fall back, resting it against the seat. He'd claimed he was tired and closed his eyes, but Mackenzie had noticed him rubbing his temples…almost as if he were in pain. When she'd asked him about it, he'd said that he was "fine" and then grinned, a hint of teasing in his response because of all of her I'm-fine retorts earlier in the day.

Those instances, along with the one from a few seconds ago, made her think there was something going on with Jace. Something he wasn't telling her. Maybe wasn't telling anyone.

When they'd been young, he'd never hidden things from her…or at least that was what she'd thought. Until the day she'd found an envelope addressed to her and slipped in with the other ranch mail. One that detailed how Jace *had* to go. *Had* to choose the rodeo over her. One that told her he was sorry.

Not as sorry as she'd been.

She led Jace toward the storage area connected to the back of the barn that held all of the seasonal equipment. She wasn't sure if they had anything usable or not, but it was worth checking before they spent money.

The ranch did well, but they were all frugal and careful to keep it that way.

She stepped into the storage room, and two figures in the corner jumped apart as if they'd been Tasered. Nick and Trista. The young couple had come on staff this summer, already dating, and had obviously just been caught, attached at the lips.

Certainly it was a kiss that no one was meant to see.

But at a guest ranch, there was no privacy.

Emma had warned Mackenzie before she'd hired the wrangler that he was already dating Trista, one of the Kids' Club staffers. So before offering him a position, she'd talked to the two of them about exactly what kind of protocol would be expected from them. What behavior was not acceptable.

They'd just blown through the details of that conversation.

"You guys." Disappointment sucked the oxygen from the room. "We talked about this when I hired Nick. You knew the rules when you came on staff."

Nick and Trista shared an embarrassed glance.

Jace stiffened at the encounter, his shoulder brushing Mackenzie's. Was he biting his tongue? Or staying out of it? Either way she felt strangely supported having him stand next to her. Having him be a witness to the situation. At least then it wouldn't be Nick and Trista's word against hers if things went further south.

Nick squared his shoulders, regret evident. "It was my fault. I'll take the blame."

"I'm so sorry." Trista teared up. "We didn't mean to. I was just putting some things away and we ran into each other in here. It wasn't calculated. I promise."

"If you give us another chance, it won't happen again." Nick added. "I love working here. Trista does, too. We both need to make money to cover our college expenses."

Mackenzie was torn between sympathy for the couple and concern for the ranch, for the livelihood of her family. If a guest had run into these two…that would have been a whole different scenario. So unprofessional. "We can't have you meeting up, accidentally or on purpose, during work. And we definitely can't have a guest—adult or child—running into you like this. Personal time should be spent together outside the ranch. Not here."

Trista covered her face with her hands. "I'm mortified."

"Keep her and let me go if you have to. I don't want Trista losing her job because of me."

Well. Mackenzie's heated upset notched down. They were just young and in love. And it wasn't like she'd caught them doing anything more…thankfully.

Normally Mackenzie would talk to Luc and Emma before making a decision about what to do in a situation like this, but things were too busy this summer. She'd have to go with her gut. And her instincts said they were just kids who'd made a mistake.

"I'm going to write this up in your employee files, and then I'm going to give you another chance. But if this happens again, you'll both be let go. Okay?"

Nods answered her, their fearful expressions subsiding.

"All right. Please go back to whatever you're supposed to be doing."

They scampered off after expressing their thanks for the second chance.

"Well, well, well." Twinkling eyes accompanied Jace's teasing. "Look who has a big ole softy heart."

"I do not."

He let loose with a deep laugh, just like he had outside, when he'd told her she couldn't ride a bull because she was a girl.

Of course he'd been joking. Jace had never been the type to say anything derogatory about women. Quite the opposite. He'd thought his mama was strong for overcoming all she had, and Mackenzie had always considered that one of his attractive qualities.

Not that she needed to dwell on any of those.

"We have to write them up. If we don't, and there's a next time, I won't have any proof. Though hopefully it won't be needed."

"Sounds good, boss."

"You can quit with the boss stuff now."

"Oh, Kenzie Rae." His scratchy drawl

lowered and strung out like honey. “I’m just getting started.”

Her sigh expanded to fill the room. “That’s exactly what I feared.”

Chapter Seven

"We keep the employee files in Luc's office," Mackenzie explained to Jace as they entered the room. She unlocked the file cabinet and removed the two folders she needed. "We use a standard form. It's on the computer." She was about to drop into Luc's chair behind the desk when she realized there wasn't a second seat. And she had promised Luc that she'd actually train Jace. "Hang on."

She went down the hall and stole a chair from the front office. When she finagled it through Luc's doorway, Jace strode over. "Let me."

"I've got it. It makes no sense for you

to take the chair with only one arm. Now, scoot so I can get this thing in here."

Jace moved out of her way, grumbling under his breath. She only caught *confounded* and *stubborn*.

Her lips pressed and bowed. Fine. Mackenzie would take those descriptions any day. She maneuvered around Jace and situated the second chair so that it was squeezed behind the desk, with hers.

After she took a seat in the rolling chair, Jace dropped into the one next to it with an agitated—and rather pouty—huff.

"I don't like being useless."

Mackenzie understood that. She'd been a much-bigger baby about a broken leg when she was a kid and had hated every cooped-up moment. "You're not. You just need a little time…to come to terms with the fact that a girl is stronger than you." She flashed him a victorious smirk. It was nice to have something up on the man—at least more than that quarter of an inch that shrank down to nothing when she went toe-to-toe with him.

"I've never doubted your toughness, Kenzie Rae. You are most certainly a force to be reckoned with."

She wrinkled her nose and rocked back in surprise.

"You don't like it when I agree with you, do you?"

"I don't know that I don't *like* it. It just surprises me."

Jace's low chuckle reignited something long forgotten and buried inside her. Attraction. Definitely the kind that should remain off the table.

The space behind the desk shrank even more when Mackenzie began clicking through folders on the computer and Jace leaned in to catch what she was doing.

"It should be in the employee-form folder… There it is. So we'll just print it off and fill it out. And then I'll have the two of them sign copies for their files so that they know what's expected in the future."

The *zip-zip* of the printer filled the quiet. Jace grabbed the sheet and handed it off to her—he wouldn't be able to fill in much with his casted hand.

Mackenzie wrote in Trista's and Nick's names, then drew a blank when she got to the part about describing the incident, because Jace had inched even closer to her, and her brain cells had taken a hike the second his shoulder had grazed hers. He smelled like high school Jace. Soap and deodorant with a hint of sweat from the day—he'd supervised the shooting range this afternoon—but that scent wasn't unwelcome. And if that wasn't the strangest thought she'd ever had…

"Trying to figure out what you're going to say?" Jace questioned.

"Um…yeah." Something like that. "I'm not exactly sure what wording to use."

"I have a few suggestions."

His humor transferred to her amused lips. "I'm sure you do." Mackenzie could only imagine what he would come up with. "I do not think Human Resources would approve."

Jace studied her profile, and she willed

her skin not to react, not to overheat, not to notice. None of which worked. "Does HR care if my boss was sabotaging my work when I first started?"

"HR doesn't take complaints like that."

Jace laughed, rich and loud and delicious, just as banging on the office door—which had a tendency to swing shut—interrupted.

"Come in," Mackenzie called out.

Jace didn't scooch back, though everything in her was screaming for him to do exactly that. They weren't doing anything wrong, but her sympathies flared for the awkwardness Trista and Nick must have felt in the storage room.

Bea poked her head inside the office. "Mackenzie? Vera sliced her hand open, and it doesn't look good."

"Coming." She popped up from behind the desk, and Jace moved to let her out.

Mackenzie jogged with Bea across the lodge lobby and into the kitchen. Red splattered the floor, the countertop, the towel wrapped around Vera's hand. She hadn't been expecting all of *this*.

"Vera, are you okay?"

The silver-haired woman was seated on the stainless-steel kitchen countertop, with her hand elevated. "I'm guessing you're not going to believe me if I say I'm fit as a fiddle?"

"Ah, no."

The woman's favorite answer to "how are you?" wasn't going to work at the moment.

"I'm sorry about this." Despite her pluck, Vera wobbled on the edge of tears. "I was cutting an avocado and the knife just went…" She shuddered.

Vera was in her early fifties and had ended up at the ranch this summer because she'd recently made some life changes. She'd told Mackenzie during her Skype interview that after living timid and afraid for a long time, she'd started taking risks—like quitting her job of twenty years to pursue new things and choosing gratefulness instead of negativity. She wanted to explore, she'd said. To stop people-pleasing and grab each day by the horns.

Probably hadn't imagined this as part of that scenario.

Joe, head chef and Wilder family member since Mackenzie had been young, brought an ice pack and applied it to Vera's wrapped hand. "This is just a war wound, honey. Every good chef has a few." He lifted his weathered, arthritis-burdened fingers, showing the white scars in his rich black skin. But after the display of calm for Vera's benefit, his eyes toggled to Mackenzie's. They held alarm, and his head gave a quick shake.

Jace stepped into the circle. Mackenzie hadn't realized he'd followed her. "I've been around my fair share of injuries and blood. Gotta be honest, Vera, I'm not sure you're even above a four on the scale for the worst stuff I've seen."

His teasing earned a watery chuckle from Vera. "Thanks a lot, bull rider. Way to kick a woman when she's down."

"Mind if I look?" Jace asked.

Mackenzie waved him forward. "As long as Vera's okay with it."

The woman inhaled and then nodded.

"Look over my shoulder and count the bins on that shelf, okay?" When she followed Jace's directions, he unwrapped the towel, quickly, efficiently, so that they could see the cut.

It was deep and gaping.

Unfortunately Vera saw it, too, and she let out a squeal of horror and swayed from her seated perch on the countertop. Jace rewrapped it quickly and then situated himself next to her, tucking a friendly arm around her shoulders as if they were two buddies, hanging out, even though he was probably keeping her upright.

"Looks like you've earned yourself some stitches. Kenzie, you driving?"

Mackenzie was in shock herself, from the amount of blood, from Jace's ability to jump in and handle the whole thing like he was a medic. From the fact that Jace… belonged. He fitted. Even after she'd tried so hard to tell him he was a round peg and Wilder Ranch was a square hole.

"Kenzie Rae." Her name wasn't a question; it was more of a command.

"Yes, of course. Let's go."

Jace kept an arm around Vera as they walked to the front of the lodge, just in case. Vera was handling the injury well at this point, but he didn't need her crumbling to the floor and adding another.

Mackenzie had jogged over to Luc's office to grab her keys. Her small Ranger pickup was parked at the lodge, which worked out well, since Jace didn't think Vera was up for one of her enthusiastic speed walks.

"You're a trouper, Vera. You're going to be just fine. Although I don't see why you have to create such a fuss over a little cut." Jace waited to see if she'd take the bait.

"You're just jealous that I'm getting all of the attention. You can't be fawned over all of the time, bull rider."

He laughed. "That's my girl." If he kept her engaged, they'd have her fixed up in no time.

Jace had liked Vera right away when they'd met. She was quick-witted, funny, positive. She'd told Jace that she used to live a painfully solitary existence. She'd been a complainer. Sad. Bitter even. And then, about a year and a half ago, she'd had an aha moment and flipped everything upside down. She'd transformed her life in gigantic, hard steps. The scariest of which had been quitting her job. She'd begun roaming, traveling, taking odd jobs as they came. And according to her, they always did. That was how she'd ended up at Wilder Ranch for the summer—on a whim.

Jace wished the woman would become friends with his mom. She could use a bright light like Vera in her life.

Everyone could.

Outside, he assisted Vera into the middle seat. Mackenzie showed up with her keys and buckled Vera in. The three of them squished into the pickup like sardines, but it was probably for the best. That way they could hold Vera up without admitting they were doing exactly that.

She kept her hand elevated and iced while Mackenzie drove.

The local hospital was very small and should probably be classified as more of an urgent-care center. No wonder Cate and Luc had driven to Denver when she'd gone into labor. Jace shuddered to think what would have happened if they hadn't.

Mackenzie dropped Jace and Vera by the entrance, then parked. When Jace offered Vera an arm to lean on, she took it as if he were escorting her to a play or the opera, all regal and proper.

Mackenzie caught up with them just inside the sliding doors. The waiting area was empty. There was no one—literally not a soul—occupying the chairs or the desk. They were open, right? It wasn't much after five o'clock. They had to be.

"You two sit and I'll see if I can find someone." They got situated while he strode to the desk and checked behind it. He had no idea what someone would be doing down there, but really, where was everyone?

"Hello? Anyone here?"

"Coming," someone called out from behind the wall flanking the reception desk. Seconds later a woman wearing scrubs covered in kittens rounded the divider.

"Ms. Silvia?"

At Jace's recognition, she went from scowl to melting. "Jace Hawke? Is that you?" She dropped items on the desk and then reached across for a hug. "It's about time you came home to visit."

"It's good to see you, Ms. Silvia."

"What are you doing here? Your mama okay?"

"She's fine. I brought in one of my coworkers. She cut her hand open pretty bad."

"Oh, sweetie. Poor thing. We'll get her fixed up. Just need you to fill out some paperwork."

"I'll do that." Mackenzie popped up and took the clipboard from the woman. "It will be workers' comp."

"I see." Ms. Silvia's narrowed gaze swept down Mackenzie as if she'd taken the knife to Vera herself, and Jace squashed a smile. It was good to have someone on his side. His team. And Ms. Silvia had always been that.

When things had been rough as a kid, he'd ridden his bike down the street to her house. She would give him a cookie or a glass of lemonade. Sit on the front step with him. She'd even hired him for odd jobs and paid him for them.

She'd been a saving grace in his childhood, especially when Dad had fought with Mom. Evan had been partial to disappearing from the house during those spats, too—or at least hiding behind loud music and headphones.

Mackenzie returned to the seat by Vera and began filling out paperwork, asking the injured woman for details as needed.

Jace leaned across the desk. "Is there any way we could get Vera back quickly? It's a pretty deep cut." Not that Jace had gotten that great of a look with all of the drama in the kitchen. But he'd seen enough to know she needed medical attention.

"I'll have our medical assistant bring her back. Dr. Bradley is just finishing up with another patient, and he's all we have on tonight. We're short-staffed." Ms. Silvia patted his hand. "You just hang tight, sweetie."

"Thank you," Jace called out as she took off, then rejoined Vera and Mackenzie, taking the seat across from them.

"Thanks for checking if they could get her in faster." Mackenzie quirked an eyebrow. "Sweetie." She added some sugar to her tone.

"You're welcome, honey." Mackenzie could bring it, as far as he was concerned. She'd been holding back from any real conversation with him. Acting as if they didn't have a past.

If she wanted to play, he'd play.

"Good thing you were here. If Vera and I would have been alone, it would be tomorrow before she got treated." Vera's eyes were closed, but a small laugh came from her. "Ms. Silvia have a crush on you?"

Jace had accused Kenzie of as much with the zip-line kid, but really… "Why? You jealous?"

She rolled her eyes.

"Silvia used to take pity on me as a kid. Throw odd jobs my way and then pay me for them. I'm pretty sure I did a horrible job at each one, but she never stopped asking me for help. And there was usually a treat of some sort involved, too. I'm sure she knew I wouldn't have had any money if she hadn't shoved some my way. But she always made me work for it."

"My opinion of Ms. Silvia is growing."

"As it should."

"What is it with females and you? In high school Mrs. Beign used to give you a hall pass all of the time, and you'd just mess around and not go to class."

Curved lips—sure to annoy Kenzie—sparked and grew. "What can I say? Women love me." He followed the quip with an I-can't-help-it shrug.

"Not all women." Mackenzie tossed him one of those sassy smiles she kept in her pocket for parting shots.

"Trust me, honey." He dropped the endearment again. "That is information I do know."

Whoops. Mackenzie had traveled into uncharted territory during this conversation with Jace, and she wanted out. Now.

"How are you doing, Vera?"

The woman's eyelids were shuttered, her breathing even. "Fine. I'm just sitting here, listening to you two bicker and flirt, wondering how I never noticed anything between you before."

Jace hooted, and humiliation consumed Mackenzie. See how quickly things got out of hand when Jace was involved? She was far more professional when the man wasn't in tow.

Ms. Silvia bustled back to the desk, and a young girl who looked annoyed to be alive met them in the waiting room. "Follow me." The deep organ notes of her greeting screamed, *I'm bored* and *I want to go home* all at once.

Vera stood. "I want you guys to come with me. That way, if I faint, you can pick me up off the floor."

"You're not going to faint." Jace popped up and wrapped an arm around her as they began walking. "You're way too tough for all of that."

"I'm not so sure about that, bull rider."

Mackenzie dropped off the paperwork with Ms. Silvia, and the three of them entered the exam room. After the medical assistant took Vera's vitals, she scampered off to hide until her next torturous human encounter.

Five minutes later a man with salt-and-pepper hair and wearing a white lab coat came in. "I'm Dr. Bradley." His teeth were perfect and oh-so-bright. His smile was AARP-commercial-worthy.

And a very single, never-been-married Vera looked as dazed as if she'd just walked into a wall. How could the handsome doctor have more of an impact on her than her sliced-up hand?

Dr. Bradley motioned to the exam table. "Have a seat. Let's get your hand checked out."

Based on the next few minutes, it was more like the two of them were going to check out each other. If Vera thought Mackenzie and Jace had been flirting, it was nothing compared to the current doctor-patient vibe. Plenty of gazing, smiling and gentle shoulder touches were exchanged. At the current rate it would take days for Vera's hand to get stitched up.

Jace leaned close enough that he could whisper under Dr. Bradley and Vera's conversation. "I feel like we're on their first date with them."

Mackenzie snort-laughed, and doctor and patient turned to investigate. "Sorry. Nothing to do with you, Vera." Although… guess that hadn't exactly been the truth.

She slugged Jace on the arm after the two turned back to their conversation. "Stop it! HR does not approve of your shenanigans."

Jace just grinned, and annoyingly her pathetic cells swooned. *Enough, traitor body. This man wrecked you once, and he can do it again far too easily.*

Dr. Bradley was telling Vera about his grown children now and his first grandson. Vera seemed to have forgotten about her hand. And maybe Dr. Bradley had, too.

Jace sank down in his chair, letting his head fall back against the wall.

"Searching for a comfortable position, Hawke?"

"Yep. Considering that we're going to be here for a while..." He studied Dr. Bradley and Vera through squinted eyes. "Weeks maybe. He's going to tell her she needs a hand replacement and lots of follow-up visits. You may want to warn your workers'-comp insurance things are about to get expensive."

Mackenzie managed to keep her amusement quiet this time. She leaned in Jace's direction, her voice a whisper. "What if Dr. Bradley has three wives, all in different states?"

"I don't," the doctor answered. "I'm widowed, actually."

For real? He'd heard her? How? Did the man have bionic ears? Of course it was Mackenzie's comment that he'd caught, not Jace's.

At least Dr. Bradley didn't look upset with her.

"I'm so sorry. Really." Could Mackenzie fit under her chair? The temptation to crawl under something was strong.

"Thank you." Dr. Bradley was gracious, nodding to accept her apology.

In her peripheral vision, Jace shook with laughter. "Stop it," she hissed, which only increased his enjoyment of her blunder.

"I'm sorry to hear that, too." Vera touched Dr. Bradley's arm with her uninjured hand. "So…you're not married…or…seeing anyone?"

Dr. Bradley's pristine white teeth flashed. "No, I'm not seeing anyone."

Go, Vera! The woman was not afraid—Mackenzie would give her that. At least Mackenzie's humiliating moment had been used for good. Vera was a woman on a mission today. She hadn't been kidding about living every moment to the fullest—no regrets.

And why shouldn't Vera go for it? If nothing came of her flirting with Dr. Bradley, she'd be on to her next adventure and job before long, and would probably never see the man again.

She had nothing to lose.

Unlike Mackenzie, who, since Jace's arrival, felt like she had everything to lose. Her sanity. Her peace. He kept inching into her space—physically and figuratively. Currently his arm was dangerously close to hers, on the armrest between them. Just that caused her skin to tingle with awareness.

The man made it too easy to remember how good it had once been between them. And way too easy to forget how he'd left.

Chapter Eight

Thirty minutes in the exam room, and Dr. Bradley and Vera were still enthralled with each other.

Jace leaned closer to her chair, still willing to risk conversation that only he could get away with. "We could be doing the chicken dance over here and they wouldn't even notice us."

"Mmm. Chicken." Mackenzie should never skip lunch like she had today. It wasn't safe for anyone when she didn't eat on a regular schedule. Like a toddler or a baby. "Trust me when I say that no one wants to see you do that."

"Afraid you'll find my moves too attractive to resist?"

"I'm afraid the doctor will think you have something wrong with you medically and want to admit you."

His mouth formed a confident, distracting arch. "I know you're laughing underneath that iceberg veneer, Kenzie Rae. I always could make you laugh."

"Could not." *Impressive comeback.* Mackenzie barely resisted an eye roll at her elementary maturity. "I can't believe I said that about—" Mackenzie nodded toward Dr. Bradley in lieu of using his name. He'd probably overhear again if she did. "You bring out the worst in me, Hawke."

"No, ma'am. I believe I bring out the best."

Maybe he had once upon a time, but not anymore.

Without warning, Jace grabbed her hand and hauled her up from the chair. "Vera, we're going to hit the vending machines. Do you want anything?"

Vera shook her head, and then Mackenzie was dragged out of the room by Jace. She should say something, do something… but before she could get her lax vocal cords functioning, the aggravating man severed their contact.

"Sorry." He stared at where their joined hands had just been. "You implied you were hungry, and…old habits die hard, I guess."

She ignored the flash of muscle memory and her on-fire fingers, reaching into the trough of hurt that this man ignited instead. "You know I'm still—"

"Don't say it," Jace interrupted her. "You're still mad at me, and I get that. You can be. But at some point you and I are going to talk. When you're ready. At some point we're going to work this out."

Mackenzie's body ached from discussing their past, even in such loose terms. "I'm not ready."

"Okay." Jace's chest deflated. "Then I'll wait. You tell me when."

"What if I never want to talk about it?"

Mackenzie hated that what had happened between them still had its claws in her.

For so long she'd wondered why he'd left the way he had. But now that she had the opportunity to find out, Mackenzie was afraid to know the truth. "I loved bull riding more than you" or "I didn't love you anymore" weren't things she could survive hearing. Even now.

"I hope that's not the case, because there are things I need to say. Things you need to understand." Jace held her gaze for a hot minute—as if driving his point home—and then turned toward the vending machines.

They walked the rest of the way in silence. He slipped money inside the snack and beverage machines, pressed some buttons, then handed her a sweetened iced tea and a package of Reese's Peanut Butter Cups.

What? How did he *do* that?

Jace scooted to the left and pressed a few buttons on the coffee machine, making a cup of brew to go with his Junior

Mints, while Mackenzie reeled from the simple gesture.

He took a tentative sip, testing the temperature as he faced her. “What’s wrong?” He touched the package in her hand. “Did I get you the wrong thing? I didn’t even think to ask. I just…”

And there was the problem—not the lack of asking, but the fact that he knew her like he did, even after so many years of separation. That he remembered something simple like what she ate or drank.

It was painful to think about what they’d once had—where they’d once been in their relationship—and where they were now.

“No, it’s fine. I’m just…” And then—ugh—her turncoat eyes filled with moisture.

Jace didn’t ask for permission, he just enveloped her in a hug, his coffee and candy held around her back, her peanut-butter cups and drink tucked between them. “I’m so sorry, Kenz.” He held her tightly, and she let her muscles sag for just a minute. Just one minute. “I’m so sorry.”

Mackenzie beat tears back with a stick while crushed against this man, who'd held her heart for so long. She really needed him to let her keep it whole this time.

"Me, too, Hawke." She forced herself to push away from him. To break the contact that had felt like home. "Me, too."

Jace had been right about the length of time they were at the hospital with Vera. The visit had lasted for hours—though thankfully not a week—because another emergency had come in. Dr. Bradley had split his time between the two patients, but eventually Vera had gotten fixed up.

In more ways than one.

She also had a date planned with Dr. Bradley for Saturday night.

Someone might as well find love, because it certainly wasn't going to be Jace anytime soon.

He was married to his work. And the only girl he'd ever loved was still angry with him.

Rightfully so.

Mackenzie parked as close to the female staff's lodging as she could get, and they unpacked themselves from her pickup. The two of them sandwiched Vera on the walk to her room and up the stairs.

"The stars are gorgeous tonight!" Vera waved her uninjured hand at the sky. "So beautiful." Reverence with a side of pain meds.

Jace shared an amused glance with Mackenzie over the woman's head. Vera's rose-colored view of the world tonight was only a smidgen more than her everyday positivity.

He waited outside the door to her room while Mackenzie settled Vera inside and made sure she had her medicine and water for the middle of the night. "Call me if you need anything. I'll keep my phone turned up." Mackenzie shut the door behind her. "Do you think she's going to be okay for the night?"

"Yep. The medicine should knock her out." They walked down the stairs. "Plus you told her to call if she had an issue.

And I'm guessing you keep your phone on every night, in case of an emergency."

Mackenzie's lips quirked. "Maybe."

"You're a pretty good boss, Wilder."

They paused near her truck. "Now you're just kissing up."

The phrase sent his mind happily skipping down memory lane. Jace definitely hadn't been doing any of that. He would have remembered.

Outdoor lights emphasized the red skin flaming at Mackenzie's obviously regrettable choice in wording. Jace wanted to jump all over that. Question if she was extending an invitation. But he knew better—Vera might get to fall in love on a whim, but he and Kenzie didn't have that luxury this time.

Not when their careers were on two different paths. Not when he was bound and determined not to hurt her again.

"I've never seen anyone fall in love that fast, and in an emergency room to boot."

Jace welcomed Mackenzie's shift in conversation. Anything to get him away from his current outlawed thoughts. “Me either.”

“She’s so happy. To think that maybe she just met her match for the first time at fifty-four years old… That’s pretty cool.”

Vera and Dr. Bradley had moved fast—Jace would give them that. But then again, life was too short to wait around and see if something happened.

Life was also too short to delay explaining to Mackenzie about why he’d left the way he had, but he couldn’t push her much faster. She needed time and he had to respect that.

“Agreed. You headed to bed?” It wasn’t that late, but he was exhausted. Mackenzie had to be, too.

“Yeah. In a minute. Need a ride?” She opened the driver’s door to her truck.

“Nah.” The guys’ lodging wasn’t much past the women’s. “It’s a nice night for a walk.”

“Okay. Good night, Hawke. Thanks for your help today.”

She was thanking him? Would wonders

never cease? Jace didn't wreck the good moment by letting any of his thoughts tumble out. "You're welcome. Night."

He watched her pickup as she drove back to the lodge, the brake lights turning red as she stopped and then parked. Why wasn't she headed to her cabin? Was she planning to leave her truck at the lodge and walk?

Mackenzie got out and took the lodge steps two at a time, then disappeared inside.

What was she doing? It was late enough that anything she had to do could wait until tomorrow, wasn't it?

Except they'd never finished the paperwork. And Mackenzie had said she wanted to follow up with Trista and Nick tomorrow. Have them sign it. And her days were so jam-packed right now, covering for Luc, that she probably wanted to get it done tonight. Cross it off her list.

Mackenzie worked harder than anyone Jace knew, and due to the toughness in his profession, that was saying a lot.

Jace followed the path to the lodge and

found Mackenzie exactly where he'd expected to—hunched over Luc's desk.

"Trying to avoid training me again, Wilder?"

She flew inches off her chair, surprise quickly morphing to confusion at the sight of him. "What are you doing here?"

"My job." He joined her, taking the chair still next to the rolling one she occupied. "Sorry if I startled you there. I should have given you some indication it was me." Even though the ranch was completely safe, a woman still had to watch out for herself. Had to keep her intuition on high alert. After the late shift stocking shelves at the five-and-dime, his mom had always walked to her car with someone else. It just made sense to be careful. "Sometimes I can be kind of an idiot."

Mackenzie's lips twitched. "I hadn't realized." She motioned to the paperwork with the pen in her hand. "You don't need to be here. I'll handle this. Just wanted to get it done tonight because tomorrow things will be crazy again—"

A loud growl interrupted her.

"Was that your stomach or a bear?"

Her laughter made Jace's previous exhaustion fade. "Guess that candy didn't count as dinner for you either. I'm starving."

She set the pen on the desk, and it rolled to the edge of the papers and stopped. "We could sneak into the kitchen. See if there's anything left from dinner or make a sandwich."

"Sounds good to me."

They abandoned the paperwork. In the kitchen, Mackenzie flipped on the lights. Thankfully the staff had cleaned up the mess from earlier. The strong smell of bleach permeated the space.

Mackenzie opened the fridge and poked her head inside. "No leftovers." She shuffled some items around. "But there's deli meat." She backed out with a couple of packages.

Jace scrounged for bread and located some choices. They each added what they wanted, including lettuce and sliced cheese they found in the fridge. Jace retrieved the mustard for himself and the mayo for Mackenzie.

"Thanks." She looked up momentarily when he handed the condiment over, almost as if she were wounded or concerned or…who knew what. Just like her expression earlier by the vending machines.

"You don't like mayo anymore?"

She squeezed it onto the bread. "I do. It just surprises me how much you remember about…me."

Like he could ever forget. All of her likes and dislikes, quirks and habits had set up camp in his brain years ago, with no plans to relocate. Jace returned the condiments to the fridge when they were finished, and retrieved the jar of pickle spears.

He turned. "Still need a pickle, too?"

"That definitely has not changed. A sandwich without a pickle is a crime." Mackenzie retrieved a spear for herself and didn't even ask if he wanted one. Because he didn't. Never had, never would. See? She knew him, too.

They cleaned up after themselves and then took their plates back to Luc's office. This time Jace dropped into the rolling chair.

"What do you think you're doing, Hawke?"

"Learning." He took a bite of sandwich and set his plate to his right so that Mackenzie had room for hers on the left. "Let me try this. That way I can help if someone else needs to have a warning added to their file." Jace took the pen and began detailing—very horribly, due to his cast—what had happened this afternoon.

Found employees canoodling in the barn. They were warned that if this happened again, they would be let go.

It looked like a four-year-old had scribbled across the paper by the time he was done. Although Ruby would have probably done a better job.

Mackenzie wiped her hands on a napkin and snatched the sheet to read what he'd written. It took her a second to decipher his handwriting. "What? No. You can't write that." A chuckle followed. "There is nothing professional about what you just wrote, Hawke."

"Why? What's wrong with it? It's true." Jace ate his sandwich while Mackenzie stole the pen and scribbled out *canoodling.* Then she must have decided the form was too messy, because she leaned over him and clicked Print on another.

And she smelled good doing it, too. Mackenzie had always rocked simplicity. Her nails were always unpainted and short, her hair wild and free. And in high school she'd smelled like that baby-powder deodorant, soap and freedom. But she must have started using a different lotion or hair product or something since he'd left, because she was this strange mix of new and old and sweet and fresh.

Jace wasn't opposed to the change.

After the printer spit out the form, she began writing, her head shaking, a smile hiding beneath the tug of her teeth against her lip. "An improper physical proximity for a work environment." She spoke as her hand scrawled much-neater letters onto the page.

"Canoodling. Exactly."

She laughed again, and something warm and forbidden rose up in Jace. He used to make her laugh all of the time, just like she used to make him. He missed that.

Mackenzie added a few more sentences between bites of her sandwich, while Jace finished off his.

"There. Good enough." She slid the paper toward him. "Can you sign on the bottom as a witness? And then I'll have them do the same sometime tomorrow."

Jace scrawled his jumbled signature, and Mackenzie's followed.

"Anything else, boss?" Jace wasn't leaving if she had more work to do.

"Nope." She finished off the last of her sandwich and brushed her fingers. "Now I'm going to crash."

"Me, too."

They returned their dishes to the kitchen, washed them and added them back to the stack. On the way out of the lodge, they flipped off lights, leaving the outside one on when they got to the front door.

"Did you have any plans tonight that were disrupted with Vera's stuff?"

Jace shut the lodge door and made sure it latched before following Mackenzie down the steps. "Just my job." He winked to show he was teasing. No need to get Mackenzie all riled up when she'd finally stopped wanting to kick him in the shins. At least that was what he assumed, based on her recent behavior. "Although, I do need to swing by and see my mom sometime. I haven't been able to check in on her as much as I'd originally thought I would while being home."

Mackenzie paused at the bottom of the steps. "The ranch is definitely greedy with a person's time. Are you sure you should be spending all of yours here?"

"Trying to shove me out again?"

"No. Just asking honestly if your time home wouldn't be better spent with your mom."

"She's working constantly anyway. The

woman's almost never at her house. Even though I've sent her enough money that she could have quit at least one of her jobs ages ago."

Mackenzie's eyes softened in the outdoor lodge lighting. "You're a good son."

He shrugged. "Not really, but I do love her."

"That counts."

"I sure hope so. I'll find a way to see her soon. And she said she's going to church on Sunday, so that will work, too."

"In the last year I've seen her at church a lot. Before that—not so much."

"I'm glad to hear that. I prayed for her over the years. She was the type to say she believed in God, but that was about it. I'm really glad to hear she's coming around." Especially with her emphysema. The disease was an eventual death sentence, though thankfully some people survived well with it for many years. And Jace was determined, somehow, to make that his mom's story.

"Thanks for your help today with Vera.

And the paperwork." The last bit was laced with humor.

"I'm happy to lend my HR expertise anytime. Are you leaving your pickup at the lodge?"

She nodded. "I'll just walk to my cabin."

"I'll walk with you."

She studied him, and then her head slowly shook. "I don't think that's a good idea. Would you do that for another staffer?"

"We just did with Vera."

"That's not the same and you know it. It's better if we're careful. Platonic."

"Boss and employee," he filled in.

"Something like that." The corners of her mouth sank like they were weighted. "Good night, Jace." She turned and walked up the hill.

She'd used his name, but it had been chock-full of sorrow and sadness.

When Jace had left town, he'd assumed that he was doing the right thing by pursuing Evan's dreams for him.

But maybe he'd been wrong. Maybe

Mackenzie had been the right choice. But it was too late to fix any of it now. Too late to go back and change his mind.

And if that didn't make his head ache with remorse, he didn't know what would.

Chapter Nine

"Burning the midnight oil?" Luc greeted Mackenzie as he walked into the front office, which was empty because everyone was watching the wranglers compete. Shovel races, a game in which one person would ride on an overturned shovel pulled behind a horse, and wrangler pickup, a game in which rider and horse race down to pick up a second passenger and then gallop back to the starting line, were both scheduled for tonight.

They'd even incorporated some of Jace's activities in the past couple of weeks—steer wrestling and cattle roping. Things hadn't gone perfectly, but the guests didn't know that. The wranglers had pulled it off and entertained the crowd.

"Burning the eight o'clock oil for sure." It was nice having her brother back—albeit part-time. Cate had been driving home at night and heading back to Denver each day to be with the babies. Luc had been alternating days between the hospital and work. Mackenzie had tried to tell him they didn't need him, that he should go be with his wife, but the truth was, they did. She hadn't done a very good job of covering his work, and they both knew it. It just wasn't the same without Luc, just like the Kids' Club wouldn't be the same without Emma.

Mom had only been able to stay a week, so Mackenzie and Emma had been helping out with Ruby, or she'd been attending the Kids' Club during the days Luc was gone.

Supposedly the twins were going to be discharged soon, and it felt like everyone was holding their breath until that finally happened.

Luc dropped into the chair at the desk, next to hers. "Did you hear about tonight?"

"No. I've been holed up in here, trying to get these last-minute reservations for August confirmed."

"We haven't had an injury around here in forever, and now all of a sudden we had Vera's, and tonight we almost had another."

"What? Who? What happened?"

"Nothing, thanks to Jace. A toddler sneaked through the railing tonight. It was so quick. He was so quick. The wranglers were racing, and they didn't see him. Jace had been sitting on the railing—because, of course, he can't compete with his broken arm—and he hopped down and scooped the boy up before he got trampled. Ran him out of harm's way. I couldn't believe it." Luc rubbed his fingertips into his forehead. "The guests were grateful and not upset. Which is great. I can't even imagine what kind of nightmare that would be if he'd gotten hurt. They said Titus is just one of those boys who moves so fast, they have trouble keeping tabs on him."

Mackenzie's stomach revolted at the thought of a child getting injured or worse on their watch, their ranch. "I'm so thankful he's okay. How would we ever live with ourselves if…?" She couldn't finish the sentence.

"I don't know. It would be horrible. I'm sure glad Jace saw it happening and rescued the kid."

"Me, too."

Luc stood and slapped a hand on her desk. "Go home, Kenzie. Get some rest. You've been working enough to cover for three people. And I'm thankful for it." He flashed a grin. "Cate just got back from the hospital, so I'm headed over to the house to see her and find out how the girls are doing."

"Okay. Let me know if there's an update."

"I will. Are you good if I go with her tomorrow?"

"Of course. It's no problem."

"Thanks, best sister in the world."

"I'm telling Emma you said that!"

His laughter echoed back to her as he exited the office.

Mackenzie finished the email she was writing and hit Send, her mind stuck on Jace the Hero. She would love to get the lowdown from him, but marching over to the guys' lodging and pounding on his door didn't appeal.

No need to draw any more attention to her relationship with Jace. The hospital visit with Vera had been bad enough. Who knew what the staff had been saying about them in the weeks since?

Mackenzie had managed to keep things between them at an employer/employee professional level since that time. And whenever a thought regarding Jace popped into her head that wasn't compliant with that plan, she followed it up with a silent he's-just-another-staff-member mantra.

Mackenzie let the computer screen go dark. If it was any other employee, she *would* contact them to see how they were and thank them. So maybe a short text to Jace wouldn't be a crime.

She snagged her phone from the desk. Mackenzie might have stopped following

Jace's career years ago, but she'd never been able to force herself to delete his number from her phone. His new-hire paperwork had confirmed it was still the same.

Heard you rescued a toddler tonight.

She added some clapping emoji.

Trying to get a raise or something? Because we can't afford your kind of hero salary, Hawke.

She hit Send and then began another text.

I'm kidding, of course. I'm very thankful you were there to rescue little Titus.

"Did you hear about tonight?" Bea popped her head into the front office, startling Mackenzie. The phone slipped through her fingers, clattering against her desk.

"I did. I'm so thankful the little guy is all right."

"Definitely. Glad I'm not over here as the bearer of more bad news."

"Hey, do you know where Jace is? I wanted to talk to him."

"I think he was heading over to his mom's. Said he needed to check on her."

Sounded like something a hero would do. And Mackenzie was sounding awfully wobbly on keeping her thoughts about Jace professional only.

"Okay, thanks."

With a wave, Bea took off. Mackenzie definitely wasn't going to drive over to Mrs. Hawke's house and stalk Jace, so she'd have to talk to him tomorrow.

Her phone rang, and she plucked it from the desk. Jace's name filled the screen.

She swiped to answer. "Things are turning to hero worship around here."

No chuckle filled her ear. "Mackenzie? This is Carleen Hawke. Jace is here, and he's sick. He says there's some pills he needs from his room there. I wasn't sure what to do, so I called you. Can you get them and bring them over?"

"Of course." Mackenzie popped up from her desk and grabbed her keys. "Tell me what they look like, where they are." While Mrs. Hawke described what Jace needed, Mackenzie hopped into her pickup and tore across the ranch toward the guys' lodging.

She took the steps two at a time and barged into Jace's room. It wasn't locked—no one bothered locking their doors, because it wasn't necessary. On the nightstand, Mackenzie found numerous pill bottles. Prescription and over-the-counter.

So the man was in pain… He just hadn't thought to mention it to her.

Mackenzie spotted the bottle Mrs. Hawke had described, and then, at the last second, decided to bring them all, just in case she'd gotten the details wrong. She made a basket with her shirt and scooped the medicines into it, then held the bundle close as she hurried down the stairs and over to her pickup truck.

"I'm on my way. Do you need to call for an ambulance? How bad is he? What's going on?"

"He says it's just a migraine, and he won't let me call anyone. I'm not even sure he's coherent enough to know I'm talking to you right now. Just come."

They disconnected, and Mackenzie raced into town.

Jace's mom lived just off Main Street, in a little yellow house that usually begged for a coat of paint and some yard maintenance, but when Mackenzie arrived, all of that had changed. The house had been painted—a nice buttercream—the bushes were trimmed and the grass had been recently cut.

Jace had been busy—or more likely, with his broken arm, he'd hired the jobs out.

Mackenzie parked and gathered the bottles again as Jace's mom came outside. "Hey, Mrs. H." She rounded the front of her vehicle.

"I'm so glad you're here. He's pretty messed up right now."

She followed Mrs. Hawke up the steps and into the living room. The scent of roast mingled with old house and what was likely an imitation version of some potent perfume.

A long flowered couch perched under the front window, and Jace was stretched out on it. He had a washcloth over his forehead and eyes.

He looked… Mackenzie didn't like it. His color was gray. He didn't remove the washcloth, didn't greet her. No teasing. Nothing. She dropped to the floor next to him.

Jace lifted the corner of the washcloth so he could peek out. "What are you doing here?"

"I brought your meds." *And I'm going to excuse your snarl because you're in pain.* "Is this the one?" She held up the prescription bottle.

"Yeah," he rasped.

She fished out a pill and took the water glass that his mom offered. "Can you sit up enough to swallow this?"

Jace moved the washcloth up to his hairline and began the slow and tedious process of lifting himself into a semisitting position with one good arm. It was strange to see him so weak. Hurting so much.

Once he was halfway upright, he froze and slammed his eyelids shut. He didn't take the pill or the water. Mackenzie stayed silent, praying for relief for him.

Jace moaned, and she scooted out of the way as he dropped from the couch, onto one hand and two knees. Then he crawled—using his elbows—into the bathroom. The door kicked shut behind him, and then she heard him lose everything in his stomach.

Mackenzie wanted to be sick with him. What was going on? She'd never had a migraine herself, so she didn't know much about them. But she hadn't realized they could take down a man like Jace and render him so helpless, so tormented. Should they call someone? Jace had mentioned seeing Dr. Sanderson for his follow-up care while he was home. Mackenzie could try him, but was that the right thing to do? Or did Jace just need to get this medicine in him?

"I've never seen him like this." Carleen sank to the armrest of the couch.

"Me either."

The seconds turned to minutes as they waited, and Jace didn't return.

"What do we do with him? I'm no good at this stuff. I never was very maternal."

"That's not true, Mrs. H. You raised two great boys." Mackenzie stood, holding on to the water and pill. "I'll check on him. Why don't you make us a cup of tea?"

Carleen's hands wrung and shook. "I can do that." A hacking cough racked her small frame, and she held on to the armrest until the fit subsided. So, the emphysema had worsened like Jace had said. Mackenzie's heart split in two. Over the years, she'd checked up on Jace's mom—dropped off some extra ranch food or a dessert when she thought of it. But in the last few months, she hadn't been by. Now she was kicking herself for that.

Carleen moved into the kitchen as Mackenzie slipped off her black-and-brown cowboy boots by the front door, then padded quietly back to the bathroom in her socks. She touched the door softly, a slight tap with the pad of her finger.

"J, can I come in?"

A groan answered. She'd take that as a yes. Inside the bathroom, he lay sprawled out, head resting on the tile. The old bathroom fan revved and then settled, its rhythm erratic.

Mackenzie sank to the floor, next to him, with her back against the wall. There really wasn't room for the two of them in here, but moving Jace right now wasn't an option.

"Think you can keep one of these pills down?"

"I'm going to try." Jace managed to raise his head off the floor, and she supported it while he popped the pill and downed a quick swig of water.

Mackenzie took the glass from him and set it on her other side. When he shifted back down, his head landed on her legs.

"Sorry." He attempted to move, but she stopped him with a hand to his forehead.

"It's okay. Just stay still." All of those don't-touch, stay-professional and don't-dip-into-the-past warnings flew out the window. And truly, they'd never really had a chance.

Mackenzie had tried so hard to view Jace as a temporary employee, but her plan most definitely had not worked. Because her concern for the man was nowhere near a platonic level right now.

Seeing him in pain flattened her. Made her want to punch a hole in the wall or call every doctor on the planet until someone offered him relief.

And those were strong feelings for a staff member. She hadn't felt any of those things for Vera when she'd sliced open her hand. Just a lot of concern. But nothing like what was roaring through her right now.

Mackenzie traced two fingers along one of Jace's eyebrows, then the other. She repeated the motion on the agony lines that were etched into his brow, while wondering how she'd gotten here…and what it would take to climb back out.

* * *

Wherever Jace currently was—and his mind was so hazy, he wasn't quite sure—he never wanted to leave. Fingers slid through his hair, past his ears, across his forehead.

He squinted, taking in the tiny square beige tiles in his mom's bathroom and Mackenzie's concern peering back at him.

"How long have we been sitting here?"

"Awhile. Long enough that your mom brought me some tea and offered me a refill." She lifted the mug in a salute and took a sip, her fingers regrettably no longer on duty.

"You hate unsweetened tea."

"*Hate*'s a strong word for something like tea. And I asked her to make it. She was so upset, I was trying to occupy her with something to do."

He let his eyelids fall shut again. The black felt cool and calm now that the terror in his head was subsiding. "She's probably cleaning the kitchen right now. That was always her go-to when she was upset.

She'd scour everything and make us pull our weight, too."

"Smart woman, when she had two capable boys. And yes, Evan was still that after the accident."

True. Evan was a world traveler now. After a few rough years, he'd stopped letting the amputation hold him back. And while that was great, Jace would never be able to completely let go of his guilt over what had happened to his brother. Because mowing was supposed to have been his chore that day, not Evan's. Something he'd admitted to no one ever. Something he'd never talked to Evan about. It had been too painful. He'd been racked with remorse and shame for years. Jace had worked through some of it with time, but that core had always remained. It was part of why he'd followed Evan's dreams for him. Because Jace was the one who'd stolen them in the first place.

Mackenzie looked so serious as she studied him. He reached up to smooth the pucker splitting her brow. "You're beautiful even when you're upset." And he didn't like being the one who'd created those worry marks.

Her head shook, but a faint smile crested. "You're crossing the line, Hawke."

"No. I would never do that." But of course he was.

"Don't make me drop your head to the floor."

He winced. "I'm sorry. I didn't mean it. I take it back."

Mom appeared in the open bathroom doorway. "Are you feeling better?"

"Yeah. I'm okay now."

The exhale she released was haggard, and she leaned against the wooden frame. He was supposed to be helping her, supporting her—not the other way around.

"Need anything? Water, food?"

"Nah. I don't even want to move yet. Don't want to mess anything up with my head, so I'm just going to chill here another minute." *On the bathroom floor, with the girl I once loved with everything in me supporting and comforting me.*

Maybe Jace would never move at all.

"Just holler if you need anything." She pushed off the door frame. "Oh, I almost forgot. Mackenzie, hon, I found a dish when I was cleaning that I think is one from the ranch. From when you dropped off food. So I'll just set it by the front door."

"Okay. Thanks, Mrs. H."

"Call me Carleen, dear. How many times have I told you that before?"

His mom left. Mackenzie studied the floor, the bathroom cabinet, the ceiling.

"You visit my mom?"

"Sometimes. Not lately, unfortunately. That's why I didn't know her symptoms were getting worse."

"Kenzie Rae." He reached up and slid a hand along her cheek before letting it fall back to his side. "What am I going to do with you?"

She destroyed him. She was so caring, so sweet and yet so feisty. She was everything he'd ever wanted and still couldn't have. Not if he wanted his life back. Jace couldn't abandon Mackenzie a second time. Couldn't hurt her like that again and live with himself. And he did want his life back. He loved the rodeo—and his brother—that much.

"I think the real question is what am *I* going to do with *you*?"

"I have a few suggestions."

"Hawke!" She whacked him on the arm, and he chuckled.

"I didn't think you'd go for that."

"I can't believe you've been having migraines like this and you didn't say anything." She'd ignored his flirting, which was good. At least one of them was keeping their head on straight today. "Is that what was going on the other times you acted strange, too? What's the deal? Is this a riding injury of some sort?"

"That was a lot of questions. I think my brain hurts again."

"Argh!" Her fingers raked through her hair, an action he'd happily take over for her.

There was no point in trying to hide anything from Mackenzie now. She'd already seen him at his worst. "I have a lingering concussion from the ride that broke my arm—" he paused "—and bruised my spleen and ribs."

"What?" She actually squeaked. If he wasn't supposed to be resisting the magnet that was Kenzie Rae, he'd tell her how cute she was.

"The head stuff... It's not going away like it has before. But then I've never had a concussion this bad. I'm fighting some vertigo. And the migraines are unpredictable."

"I wonder if tonight's was because you rescued that little boy. From the movement?"

"Maybe."

She was quiet for a good long while. "Why didn't you tell me?"

"I didn't want to give you any extra reasons to kick me off the ranch."

"Can you ever be serious?"

"I am being serious. Kind of. I suppose I didn't want you to know how messed up I was. It's easier if people just think it's the arm. That's visible. That makes sense. I hate that the concussion isn't getting better. At least not fast enough for me. It makes me feel like a wuss. Guys don't quit for a concussion. They don't quit for anything. Some of them have a busted Achilles tendon and they keep riding. We all do it."

"Well. That's just dumb."

He laughed.

"Aren't concussions a really big deal? Isn't there some disease that can come from too many?"

"Sometimes. Chronic something or another. CTE for short. But that's not what's going on with me."

"Good. Says who?"

He grinned, crossing his casted hand over to latch onto her arm and rub a thumb along her soft skin. "Worried about me, are you?"

An eye roll answered.

"Doc Karvina is my rodeo doc, and he's never implied its anything close to CTE." *Just that I should stop competing before that becomes a reality for me.* "And I saw Dr. Sanderson in town, and he said I'm making improvements. The spleen and ribs are pretty much good to go. The arm still needs time." Waiting was the worst part. Instant healing would be so much more preferable. "Overall I'm a specimen of health."

"Did either doctor say they could do anything about your sassy mouth?"

Humor surfaced. "They did not mention that."

"Just…" Mackenzie huffed. "Take care of yourself, okay? This sport… It isn't worth your life."

"I will. I always do. I'm not going to do anything stupid." Jace would wait until he healed before he got back up on a bull. Or at least until the majority of his symptoms subsided.

"Good." All of that concern written across her pretty features almost did him in. Wasn't he supposed to *not* be causing the woman pain and suffering this time around?

"You going soft on me, Wilder?"

Mackenzie studied him, those mesmerizing gray depths full of all kinds of emotion he no longer had the right to. “Maybe. And if that’s not a problem, I don’t know what is.”

Chapter Ten

Mackenzie stowed the rafting supplies in the storage area at the back of the barn. She'd just returned from taking a group, and it had been glorious to get out of the office and outside. But while her favorite activity usually energized her, today she was dog-tired.

In the last two weeks she hadn't been off duty for more than an hour or two at a time. Even her Saturdays had been filled with Wilder Ranch work—issues, planning, the big Fourth of July celebration last week that was always a hit.

The only escape she had managed was for church on Sundays. At least she'd had that. And she'd needed it. She'd needed that break, that minute to remember that taking care of everything at the ranch wasn't all on her shoulders.

Because it had begun to feel that way.

Why, she wasn't quite sure. Emma was doing her job and more, even with her wedding being only ten days away. And Jace had been a huge help, too. But somehow Mackenzie still felt…alone in all of it.

The twins were finally being discharged tomorrow, so Luc's world was going to get even busier. Emma was about to get married and become a wife and a mom all in one instant I-do moment. And once Jace healed, he'd most certainly go back to bull riding.

Mackenzie couldn't shake the notion that she was being left behind once again. And she didn't like feeling sorry for herself. Didn't like this weight strangling her.

At least the campout was tonight, and many of the guests had signed up for it. Which meant that she should have a night to relax, since she wasn't in charge of that.

Sure, she'd be around in case of any emergencies, but at least the evening would allow her to chill.

After organizing, she walked over to the lodge. Jace was sitting on the front steps, almost as if he'd been waiting for someone. Her? Strange. They'd been so well behaved since the migraine encounter. No more touchy-feely. No more diving into the depths she'd promised herself she wouldn't go near.

He hadn't even pressured her to talk about the past. If this was the calm in the middle of the storm, Mackenzie wanted to rent a room and stay here.

"Anyone ever tell you that you work too much, Wilder?"

She dropped down beside him. "Anyone ever tell you that you stick your nose in other people's business too much?"

His head cocked. "Nope."

"Well, they should. If you must know, taking guests white-water rafting does not qualify as work to me." The icy-cold splash of water misting her, the thrill of the next big drop. She loved every second of it.

"I feel the same way about the shooting range. I just got back from supervising that." He nudged her shoulder with his. "You look like you could use a night off."

"Maybe."

"Definitely. So you should be thankful I finagled one for you."

"Huh?" She glanced at him. "What do you mean?"

"I mean I talked to the boss—"

"I am the boss," Mackenzie interrupted, pathetically relishing Jace's chuckle.

"Don't I know it. I meant your twin. And he's on my side. He's home tonight and agrees that you need to take the evening off. He said, and I quote, 'If Mackenzie takes a night off, it will lessen my guilt for how little I've been here lately.' Luc said he'd be on call, in case of emergency, for the campout tonight. And I have just the thing planned."

If Mackenzie was getting a night off, she intended to sleep. Well, first she'd put on a movie—*Pale Rider* or another one of her favorite Westerns—and then she'd conk out on the couch. Who said her life wasn't just as exciting and full of new adventures as the lives of everyone around her?

"I'm tired, Hawke." She barely resisted closing her eyes and dropping her head onto his shoulder. And that was saying a lot, since she'd been nothing but careful around the man.

He switched to the step behind her and began rubbing her shoulder with his non-casted hand. Her neck lagged forward, her head barely hanging on. "You're really going to put me to sleep now."

He switched shoulders. "I know how tired you are. Maybe we should do it another night."

Her curiosity perked. "What's 'it'?"

"A thank-you."

"For what?"

"For checking on my mom all of these years."

What would that be? "You got me boots?"

"No, ma'am." His drawl stretched out,

and his fingers continued to dig into her tired muscles. She moved his hand an inch to the left, and he blessedly continued. "Something you asked me about."

"Hmm." Mackenzie couldn't think. Didn't really want to right now. After this little massage, she'd crawl into bed and not come out until morning.

"Something involving a bull."

Her senses woke up, and she flipped around, causing his hand to drop. "You're going to teach me how to ride a bull?"

"Not a live one."

"What other kind are there?"

"Mechanical."

Mackenzie analyzed. If she said no, she wouldn't get to try at all, because she didn't think Jace was going to let her do the real deal. Unless…! Unless she proved that she could handle it. Then maybe she could convince him.

"A little wussy but I'll take it."

He laughed, and it registered in her stomach like comfort food. "Are you sure?

If you're exhausted, it's probably not the best timing."

"My energy has suddenly returned to me."

"Okay. But the offer stands if you'd rather reschedule."

Mackenzie suddenly wanted nothing more than to get out of here. "I'm game. Let's go make me a champ."

Jace had wanted to thank Mackenzie, not make her pass out cold on the drive to his friend's place. Her head had fallen back against the seat during the drive, her shoulders drooping lower with each mile. She'd changed into jeans, along with boots and a vintage T-shirt that had a black-and-white cow's mug on the front wearing a red bandanna. Equal parts cute and distracting. The woman was like a baby lulled to sleep, and now he didn't have a clue what to do with her.

He'd heard of the advice not to wake a sleeping baby, but a sleeping Kenzie Rae was a tad more confusing.

Jace had parked at the end of Colby's drive and not headed in yet, trying to figure out what to do, kicking himself for not knowing better than to have waited and taken her on another day. Kenzie had told him she was exhausted, and she hadn't been lying.

If he turned around and drove back to Wilder Ranch, would she be upset? What was more important? Sleep? Or a night away?

The woman had been working so hard lately, and the Fourth of July holiday last week had been even busier than usual, with all the ranch had done to celebrate that. Wilder Ranch kept Mackenzie running. Jace, too. When he'd first gotten injured, he'd assumed that waiting to heal would just about kill him. But the fast pace of his temporary job had fixed that for him.

In exactly one week his cast would be coming off. After that he'd be hitting physical therapy at a run. And then he'd be back to bull riding by September for sure. Hopefully before.

He was more than ready. But a good chunk of him was going to miss Wilder Ranch. Miss the woman next to him whose heavy, openmouthed breathing was edging toward a snore.

Maybe that should turn him off, but it didn't. He liked seeing Mackenzie relaxed. He liked it even more that it was with him.

A month ago this scenario would never have happened.

"Hawke, are you watching me sleep?" Her steel-gray eyes popped open. "Creepy!"

"More like I was watching you drool and snore." She hadn't done either, but her look of horror and panic made the jab worth it.

"I do not drool when I sleep." She swiped a hand across her lips, checking, and his gaze stalled and stuck.

He'd edged closer while analyzing whether to let her sleep, and now it would only take the slightest lean to test out his theory about her kisses and whether they were as good as he remembered.

You're thanking her, not taking advan-

tage of her tired, vulnerable state. Jace forced his body back to the driver's seat.

"Where are we? What are we doing sitting here?"

"We're at my friend Colby's. I was trying to decide what to do with you."

"Where to hide my body?" She scanned their surroundings. "The middle of that field over there would probably work."

He laughed. "Do you want to go home? I feel bad dragging you out here when you're so exhausted."

"Actually, the nap helped." Her shoulders inched up sheepishly. "I feel rested. Sorry I conked out though."

"The two-hour ride was pretty boring without anyone to talk to."

"Two hours?" She sat up straighter, took in the rock formations and evergreens that lined the drive. "Where exactly *did* you take me? I've been asleep that long?"

"I'm kidding. It was only about forty-five minutes."

"Oh." She whacked him on the arm. "If you're trying to thank me, you should probably tone down the jerk and up the doting, adoring admirer."

"Noted." If only sparring with Mackenzie was a full-time career. Jace would have job security for life. "You ready, old woman? Or do I need to get you home in time for *Wheel of Fortune*, *Jeopardy!* and a TV dinner?"

She flashed a sassy smile. "I'm ready. You're going to be sorry you ever started this with me, Hawke."

He had no doubt she was right.

Mackenzie climbed out of the passenger seat of Jace's old beater truck. It was funny to her that he didn't get a newer vehicle. Based on his career successes, he should certainly have the money. But then again material things had never appealed to him. At least not to the younger version of the man.

Take today for instance—his boots and jeans were worn, his T-shirt advertising some rodeo, his baseball cap perfectly broken in. And Mackenzie was not, for one second, going to admit those things looked good on him.

At least not out loud.

Colby had a simple but well-kept spread. A ranch house and two outbuildings were on the property, some bikes and other toys outside. The front door opened, and a young man bounded in their direction. "Ace, how's it going?"

"Ace?" Mackenzie questioned.

Humor twisted Jace's mouth. "An announcer coined the unimaginative nickname once, and the guys never let it go. It's stuck ever since."

Jace and Colby shook hands and did that one-arm-man-hug thing.

"Mackenzie, this is Colby. He retired from riding a few years back and now gives private lessons to kids, along with raising a brood of his own."

She shaded her eyes against the sun. "It's nice to meet someone who's part of Jace's life since he left Westbend. I assume you have some stories you can tell me."

Jace groaned. "I'm regretting this already and you're not even up on the bull yet."

"Yes, ma'am." Colby's full-of-mischief grin promised plenty of dirt. "That I can do. We can discuss over dinner. Les has some food in the Crock-Pot for tonight. She's working right now."

"Colby's wife is a nurse," Jace explained. "Not sure what she saw in his sorry hide."

"Me either." Colby chuckled and slapped Jace on the back. "Come on." A smattering of kids flew out the front door and chased after them as they made their way to one of the outbuildings. Two blonde girls and one blond boy, and they all looked under the age of four—maybe five.

Colby and his wife had their hands full for sure.

"Whacha doing?"

Mackenzie slowed her steps to match up with the little boy who had sidled up next to her. "I'm going to ride a mechanical bull. What are you doing?"

Two fingers slid between the boy's lips, and he spoke around them. "I'm thwee. I don't know what I'm doing." He took off like a shot and caught up to his sisters.

Cute kid.

Colby slid open the large doors on the gray building, and the three of them stepped inside. The mechanical bull was in the middle of a ring, with padded cushion surrounding it.

"Where's the real bull?"

"Out in the pasture." Colby glanced at Jace, amused. "You've got your hands full with this one."

"I already told you that's not happening, Wilder."

"Fine." She gave an exaggerated huff. It had been worth a try. Maybe there was a chance in the future, if she behaved herself. Or now that she'd met Colby, she could always go around Jace and ask him. "I'll take what I can get."

"Sure hope you know what you're doing, Ace. She's a firecracker. I gotta go make sure the kids haven't gotten into any trouble in the last minute, so I'll see you two later. Hopefully with all of your limbs intact."

* * *

Colby's parting statement didn't fill Jace with confidence. He still wasn't sure exactly what he was doing here with Mackenzie. He'd wanted to thank her for checking up on his mom over the years. With most women that would be chocolate or flowers. With Mackenzie? Something that could break her neck.

And since there was no way he was putting her on a live bull, this option was second best. If he didn't teach her, didn't help her, she'd go find someone else, out of spite, and then really get herself injured. At least he had that thought to comfort him.

But the woman had better not get hurt on his watch.

Mackenzie had hopped over the perimeter of the floor mats and was now touching the mechanical bull as if it were a live animal. "Let's do this." She climbed on and shot him a let's-go-already look.

"You're crazy. I'm going to teach you some things first so that you don't get booted right off and hurt yourself."

"Okay, but how hard can it be? Just… stay on. Right?"

His jaw unhinged, and then she pealed with laughter. Her head tipped back, hair flowing with it. Gorgeous, horrible woman.

"That was even better than your girls-can't-ride-bulls comment!"

Jace shook his head, lips twitching. Mackenzie was definitely a force to be reckoned with. And seeing her happy, teasing him… He liked all of that a bit too much.

"What's first, coach?"

Jace approached. "Put this on." He'd gotten her a glove that would fit her smaller hand so that her knuckles didn't blister or bleed. Because knowing Mackenzie, she wouldn't quit if things didn't go her way the first time. "Then slide your hand under the rope, palm up. Line up your pinkie finger along the backbone." Mackenzie did everything he said like an old pro. "Good. You want to stay up on the bull and use your legs to hold on. Make sure you stay centered."

Mackenzie scooted toward the rope, got situated.

"Use your free hand to stay balanced, and try to keep your upper body relaxed. When the bull tips down and forward, push your knees and heels into the bull and lean back. You want to shift your weight opposite of the movement. If the bull dips back, then lean forward." That was generalizing things, but he had to start somewhere.

"Makes sense."

"We're probably just going to have to try it so you can get a feel for it. Then we can work out the kinks."

Right now Jace didn't even exist to Mackenzie. She was in full-concentration mode, full-experience mode. It only upped her attractiveness. He'd always loved her adventurous spirit.

"I'm going to start you off slow so you can get the feel of it."

Mackenzie raised her left arm. "Okay. I'm ready."

Jace's gut sank to his boots. Why had he started all of this again? After a quick prayer that the woman wouldn't get hurt, he manned the controls. Mackenzie handled a few dips, but then a spin knocked her off. She popped up quickly and climbed back on before Jace even had the chance to check on her.

"You okay?"

"Yep. I just lost it on that spin. How do I stop that from bucking me off?"

"Keep your legs tight and shift the opposite way, but then you have to be ready and adjust for the next move or it will still toss you."

"Okay." Mackenzie nodded and raised her arm. "Let's go again."

The next ride was much better. Jace increased the difficulty as she went again and again, stretching her time, her skill. The woman was fierce. Every time she got thrown, she climbed back up immediately. There was no complaining. No lollygagging.

"Keep your legs tight. It's easy to focus

on just the upper body, but your legs are where your strength is."

She stayed on the longest for the next ride. Just shy of eight seconds.

"Argh! I was so close." Mackenzie remounted. "Make sure you make it hard enough to count."

Jace was controlling the speed and variation of the mechanical bull. "Trust me, I have not been taking it easy on you." He'd known she would never put up with that. Watching her get pummeled over and over again was torture, but at least she was getting better with each ride.

At her nod, he started the machine again. The mechanical bull dipped forward, back, then spun, and Mackenzie shifted with each movement. She stayed balanced and up on her rope.

"You're almost there. Six, seven, eight." Jace whooped in celebration just as Mackenzie went flying across the padding like a plastic bag caught in a gust of wind.

That had been a hard hit. He switched

the bull off and scrambled over to her. This time she didn't get up immediately, didn't make much noise at all.

The glove she'd been wearing was five feet away from her, and she was flat on her back, with a hand over her forehead. Had it knocked her out?

He moved her arm to her side. "Are you okay?"

"That was amazing." She sat up, eyes wide and bright. "Let's do it again."

Jace crashed from his kneeling position to sitting on the mat. "You're going to be the death of me, Kenzie Rae. I thought you'd gotten hurt, and I was kicking myself for letting you do this."

"Don't kick yourself. This was a good thank-you gift." Mackenzie looped arms around her bent knees. She was the kind of pretty that hollowed him out and made him want the life he'd given up for good. Jace might be leaving town again, but Kenzie Rae would always own a piece of him. There was just no one like her.

"You're welcome. I think."

"This isn't the real thing, but it's pretty addicting."

"It is. And the real thing is so much better."

"Huh. Crazy." Her tone was dry. "That must be why I asked you for that."

"Maybe someday." What? Absolutely not. This woman made him say yes to things that shouldn't even be considered. "I take that back."

"Too late! You can't take it back."

Jace tugged his baseball cap lower in lieu of digging an even bigger hole.

"I can see how you'd have a hard time giving this up." She nodded toward the mechanical bull. "If your concussion doesn't improve… Well, I can't imagine how awful that would be for you."

"It would kill me to give up riding." Not that Jace was going to worry about that. His head would get better. Not competing wasn't an option for him, so it had to. He wasn't perfect yet, but he was improving with time, and that gave him hope.

But with the way Mackenzie was talking… She knew he was going back no matter what, right? She'd asked him to be careful, and he'd said he would. Surely she didn't think—

"Ace!" Colby bellowed from the doorway as he strode their way. "Is she still alive?"

"And kicking." Mackenzie answered Colby, popping up as if she hadn't just been beaten down by the machine numerous times. As if she hadn't slept like a comatose woman the whole drive here.

Adorable weirdo.

"She did okay…" Jace pushed up from the mat, adopting the most serious face he could muster. "But she needs a lot of work."

"Hey! I did amazing!"

"And she needs to tone down her overconfidence."

"Jace Hawke, you're just upset that I did so well because you don't want to let me ride a real bull."

True.

"Let's get some dinner in you two."

At Colby's suggestion, Jace wiggled his fingers. "Sounds good. I could use a break. I'm getting sore from running the controls."

"Hawke! You're a jerk." Mackenzie poked him in the chest. "Just for that I want another go after dinner."

Great. He'd just started relaxing that she'd survived unscathed, and the woman wanted to get back up on the bull.

But then again Jace couldn't exactly blame her, since all he wanted to do—despite his uncooperative body—was exactly the same thing.

Chapter Eleven

"Who hasn't had their makeup done yet?" Emma's friend Abby scanned the cabin living room—currently being used as wedding-prep central for the women—hungry for her next victim.

Mackenzie had been standing—okay, hiding—near the wall next to Emma's bedroom. Leaning against it like the beams would crumble without her support. Praying she didn't spill something on her rust-orange bridesmaid dress while snacking on the fruit and other appetizer items filling their small dining table. Laughing when it fitted. Smiling at the right parts. Generally trying to become one with the wall and avoid notice from The Primpers in the room.

Emma had two friends helping out with hair and makeup—Abby and Kim. They'd been working tirelessly, and Mackenzie had been avoiding them with just as much effort.

"Mackenzie!" Abby zeroed in on her.

Avoid eye contact! Avoid!

"I'll go light on you. I promise."

Mackenzie's noggin shook like a bobblehead on a car dash. "I'm good, really. I don't think anyone is expecting me to wear makeup, when I never do."

Abby rounded the couch and curled a hand around her biceps, dragging her to the makeup-torture zone. "But that's exactly why we *should* do it. At least a little. Just to highlight those gorgeous cheekbones. I've been dying to get my hands on you for years. You're so naturally beautiful, you'll hardly need a thing. Just a few touch-ups here and there. Trust me. This won't hurt a bit."

Abby gave Mackenzie a slight nudge

to get her to drop to the couch cushions, then sat on the coffee table, facing her. She picked up a fat makeup brush and went to work like some kind of master painter.

What was wrong with her face the way it was? Mackenzie swallowed her protest. *For Emma. I'm doing this for Emma.* Not that Emma cared one iota what she looked like today. Her sister's eyes would be on Gage and Hudson—with cartoon hearts spilling out, no doubt.

Abby worked quickly—Mackenzie would give her that. Lip gloss, eye shadow, mascara. The items came at her like bullets.

"Oh, I have the perfect idea for your hair!" Kim's squeal came from behind the couch.

Mackenzie winced. She'd been hoping to at least avoid the hair station.

After Abby finished, Kim directed Mackenzie over to a dining room chair so that she had better access. Bobby pins scraped her scalp as the sound of women filled the room. Emma, being herself, had invited most of the women in the county to get ready with her.

Okay, that might be a slight exaggeration. But with the photographer, and Gage's mom and sister in the cabin, along with their mom, Cate, the twins, Ruby and The Primpers, things were crowded.

Everly and Savannah didn't mind though. They'd been passed around plenty and had slept through most of the commotion.

The girls had been home from the hospital for nine days, but Mackenzie had only held each of them for a few sporadic minutes in that time. They were tiny rock stars and had a following of groupies—both friends and family—vying for their attention. Mackenzie had stayed back regarding that, too, because she wasn't the baby-whispering type. But those moments connecting with her new nieces had still definitely been good.

One day she'd take them out on rides like she did Ruby. Or they'd climb trees like she and Ruby had sneaked off to do this week, during the hubbub of the babies' arrival. Usually Emma was the aunt who spent more time with Ruby, but she'd been busy with wedding prep lately, so Mackenzie had quietly stepped into that role. She'd made sure Ruby wasn't forgotten, checking in on her, stealing her away when work allowed.

And Mackenzie had enjoyed every second. Turns out her niece liked to adventure as much as she did.

Another bobby pin tore off a chunk of her scalp. "Kim, I could probably do my own hair." *Since I've been managing it for the last twenty-five years.* "I'm sure you have other people to help." *Please.*

"I don't actually. You're the last one!"

Mackenzie resisted another argument. Instead she closed her eyes, straining to find some peace in the midst of the attack on her skull.

Hopefully Jace had been able to do the same after completing the guest turnover this afternoon. He'd been up late last night with another migraine and had been disgruntled about it this morning because it had been the first in a long while. Every time he thought he had them beat, another appeared out of nowhere to derail him. And the vertigo still plagued him at times, too.

Despite those setbacks, he'd begun physical therapy once his spleen and ribs had healed, and now that his cast was off, the arm was included, too. He was obviously preparing to go back.

But at the same time, he'd told her he wouldn't do anything stupid. Which, in her mind, meant he'd heal fully before returning.

So what did that mean?

If his concussion hung around, would he retire? No one could fault him for that. He'd had a long, successful career. He could easily move on and do something else. Find a new passion. No one could ride bulls forever—their bodies would eventually give out.

Would he stay if he didn't get better? And if he did...what did that mean for them?

Was there a "them"? Mackenzie wasn't

sure she was okay with that term popping into her brain. Though the man had certainly been sneaking into her thoughts and her world a lot lately. It was so easy to lapse back into old habits with him. To remember why she'd fallen for him the first time around.

Mackenzie still didn't know why Jace had left the way he had. And she still both wanted and didn't want to know. Though the first option was gaining momentum.

Oohs and aahs caused her to open her eyes.

Emma had come out of her bedroom in her wedding dress. The living room of ladies highly approved, based on the exclamations and tears.

Rightfully so.

Emma's dress had delicate spaghetti straps and flowers along the bodice that dripped onto the long, flowing skirt. She was a woodland creature with her hair curled and loosely pulled back on the sides, sprays of flowers tucked into the do.

She was a vision. Striking and glowing and gorgeous.

Mackenzie might not love all of the changes happening around Wilder Ranch, but seeing Emma so happy made the growing pains worthwhile. She couldn't imagine a better match for her sister. Gage's world revolved around Emma, and she'd brought him back from the land of cranky and stoic after his ex-wife had done a number on him. The two of them were a perfect pair.

"Aunt Emma, does your dress twirl like mine?" Ruby was in a white flower-girl dress, and she spun in a circle, enthralled with the way the skirt flared.

"Let's see." Emma's eyes twinkled as she joined in. The moment was sweet, and the photographer must have agreed, because her camera sounded repeatedly as she captured each frame.

Emma handled the attention that came with her wedding day like a fairy-tale princess, all calm and gracious. If Mackenzie were in her shoes, she'd need boots, first off, and then a large boulder to hide behind.

If the right match existed for her, Mackenzie hoped her someday wedding wouldn't include all of this…fussing.

"All finished," Kim announced.

"Thank you." Mackenzie forced the appreciation through clenched teeth and then slunk off to the bathroom to investigate the damage.

"I don't even look like myself." She pressed over the sink, leaning close to the mirror. There she was…underneath all of the shiny, glimmery concoctions. With a tissue, she dabbed away some of the lip gloss, lightening it, then swabbed gently at the eye shadow—which, thankfully, was a soft color. Mackenzie didn't want to mess anything up so much that she ended up back in the makeup hot seat, so she quit meddling. The slight adjustments helped. She used the small hand mirror to check her hair. It was actually cute—not that she would ever take the time to do it again.

Waves were caught up at the nape of her neck, casual and stylish.

She set the mirror down and met her reflection again. "It's a wedding. You're supposed to be dolled up. And this is all for Emma." The affirmation made her mouth quirk. Hopefully no one could hear her crazy talk through the door. Mackenzie squared her shoulders. She could manage to wear the makeup and leave the hair through the wedding and reception. And then after she'd reward herself with a T-shirt, sweats, pizza and a Western with lots of gunfights.

She exited the bathroom to find everyone getting ready to either walk or ride down the hill to the lodge.

"I can walk." She volunteered to let some of the others hop in vehicles, since she was wearing cowboy boots with her dress—*thank you, Emma, for that saving grace.*

"I'll go with you," Mom said, also taking Ruby's hand. "Come with us, kiddo, but let's lift up your dress while we walk, so it doesn't get dirty."

The perfect summer-evening temperature drifted along Mackenzie's skin as they strolled, and Ruby chattered excitedly about her "fruffy" dress and light-pink-painted fingernails. Scents of grass and dirt and ranch swirled, comforting. The wedding had been scheduled for after dinner because they'd needed time to set up and get ready, but that meant a cooler temperature and twinkle lights—Emma's favorite. Both wins.

When Ruby spied Luc near the entrance to the lodge, she dropped the skirt of her dress and took off at a run.

"So much for keeping the hem clean." Mom's wry comment was spiked with humor, taking years off her already young-looking features. Her hair was a shade darker than Mackenzie's—more of a light brown—but it held some of the same wave. If not for her mother's autoimmune disease that flared in Colorado's fluctuating climate, Mackenzie had no doubt that her parents would still be living here, running

Wilder Ranch. "Reminds me of another little girl I once knew."

"Except I would have thrown a fit about the dress."

"True. I didn't know how amazing grandbabies were. Didn't realize what I was missing until Ruby and Hudson came along. And now we have the twins, too."

And none from me. Not that Mackenzie was overly maternal. She wasn't. And maybe that was why no one thought she had that ache inside her, too—for a husband, for kids, for a family of her own.

But she did. It was dull and distant, but there. And ever since Jace's reappearance, that dull, distant ache had been making itself known with troublesome throbs and sharp, shooting pains.

Jace slipped into a seat for the ceremony at the last second. He and the other staff had handled the turnover today so that the Wilders could prepare for the wedding. A few small issues had sprung up throughout the day, leaving him running behind. But they'd figured things out and managed not to bother any of the Wilder clan.

Thirty minutes ago he'd hustled over to the guys' lodging to get ready. He'd jumped in the shower and then thrown on his best jeans and a short-sleeved button-up shirt. His hair—too long and in need of a cut—was still slightly damp.

Emma had made it clear that the wedding was to be casual, and he'd taken advantage.

Music started, and Jace swiveled with the rest of the crowd, toward the back of the grass aisle. *Sweet mercy.* His windpipe closed off so fast, he barely managed not to hack and cough, and cause a scene.

There was most definitely nothing casual about Kenzie Rae.

She walked down the aisle with Luc, confident and relaxed, stunning times a million. The color-of-changing-leaves orange dress she wore accentuated slight curves, and her muscular legs tapered into cowboy boots. She turned at the front, a small batch of flowers in her hands, and watched for Emma.

Mackenzie had on makeup. The effect sent Jace bumping into the back of his chair. She was a knockout. And yet…he was partial to the girl underneath all of that sparkle and shine.

The one who rode faster than him and could probably beat him at most anything. The one who managed to siphon the oxygen from his body with just a glance.

Tuck away her jaw-dropping beauty, and Mackenzie was still a force to be reckoned with—strong and funny, vulnerable and loyal.

And Jace was the idiot who'd let her go. The same idiot who planned to repeat his actions all over again soon.

Not that Mackenzie was anywhere near *his* this time around.

Ruby came down the aisle next. She paused to wave at Jace, and he winked at her. She'd quickly wormed her way into his heart. There was something about Ruby and her bubbly personality that drew people in. Jace had only lasted a few days at Wilder Ranch before joining her fan club.

She took her time heading down the aisle, doling out precisely three flower petals to each row. When she finally reached the front, she high-fived Mackenzie. When the guests laughed at the gesture, Ruby took a bow.

Charmer.

Next came Emma on her dad's arm.

He must have said something to Mackenzie after releasing Emma's hand, because she looked like she was fighting amusement.

Mackenzie had always been a daddy's girl. What had the man thought when Jace left town after high school? He was afraid to find out. Jace had always respected Wade Wilder. Always wished his own father had been even a quarter of the man.

Things progressed quickly once Pastor Higgin began the ceremony. When they repeated the vows, Gage choked up numerous times while promising to love Emma forever. And then again when she promised the same back to him, her voice clear and strong, her tender gaze glued to the man holding her hands in a grip so tight, it looked like it might hurt her.

Jace didn't know Gage very well, but if ever there was a man in love, who desperately needed the person across from him and looked as if he'd been granted a second chance in life, it was him.

Mackenzie discreetly attempted to wipe under her lashes, but Jace caught the movement because he couldn't keep his attention from wandering in her direction over and over again during the ceremony.

After Gage and Emma were declared husband and wife, they kissed, then scooped up one-year-old Hudson on their way back down the aisle.

An instant family, just like that.

But families like the Wilders didn't grow on trees. Jace knew. He'd practically forced himself into theirs in high school. He'd loved everything about the way they operated as a unit. Teased each other. Worked hard, played hard.

After everyone had been dismissed from their rows and began mingling, Jace sought out Mackenzie. She was a magnet for him. He couldn't resist being near her, even if the end of that was too close for comfort.

"Kenzie Rae." At her name, she turned from the punch bowl, a dainty glass cup in her hand that was in stark contrast to the strong, tanned woman. The dress she wore—no doubt while grumbling—only accentuated her toned arms.

"Hawke." She sipped her punch. "How did it go this afternoon?"

"Fine. A few issues, but we handled it."

"What went wrong? Was it something with the McBanes? Because she said she wanted to talk to me yesterday, and with all of this going on, I totally forgot."

"No. Mrs. McBane only had good things to say. She wanted to rebook for next year. She didn't realize that we give everyone the opportunity to do that before they head out. So she was fine. You just can't handle not knowing everything that's going on around here, can you?" Or was it that

Kenzie didn't trust anyone but herself to manage things?

"That's not true." Mackenzie tried to take another drink of punch, but she'd already emptied it, since it held about as much as a thimble. Jace took it from her, refilled it and then returned it to her. She thanked him.

"It is true," he continued. "There was a chip in the tile in Cabin Nine. Boone and I finagled a fix as best as we could. It should hold through this week, but then we probably need to get a maintenance check on it." Evan was the one who had any fix-it skills in their family, but Jace had muddled through.

He could have called his brother to ask for advice, but he hadn't because he'd been avoiding Evan lately. Pretty much since the injury. Evan had called a number of times, but Jace had either missed the attempts or dodged answering.

He just wasn't sure what his brother was going to say...or if he was going to tell Jace to quit. To retire.

And Jace really didn't want to hear it right now. Not when he was bent on getting better. Positive attitude went a long way, and he refused to entertain any other thoughts right now.

"That's not bad. So everything went okay, then?"

"Yes. Everything went fine." Only Mackenzie would be talking shop at her sister's wedding. "If I thought I'd detected some tears from you during the cere—"

"You'd be wrong." Her reply was quick, humor flaring so fast, he almost missed it. "Allergies. They were really kicking up tonight."

"Ah. And yet they seem better all of a sudden."

Those glossy, distracting lips of hers broke into a curve. "Amazing, right? What were you doing watching me anyway, when Emma's the bride? She looks so stunning, I'm surprised everyone wasn't blinded by her beauty."

"She does look beautiful. But she's no you." Jace didn't temper his words. He should be able to speak the truth at a wedding, shouldn't he?

Based on the confusion and softness cresting Kenzie's features…maybe not.

"J." Mackenzie's eyes shimmered—with tears or "allergies," he couldn't be sure. "That was sweet."

He waved a hand over her hair. "I like what you've got going on here."

"Thanks, though you'll probably never see it this way again. Emma's friend did my makeup—" she motioned to her face "—and I didn't have the heart to fuss. I was trying to be all Team Emma for the wedding. No complaining. Whatever she wants."

"You look like a celebrity. Like I should be standing in line to get your autograph. But I'm actually partial to the girl who treats makeup like a venomous snake and doesn't know what to do with the smoky-powder stuff covering your eyelids. I like that Kenzie Rae a whole lot."

"I—" She faltered. "That's the nicest thing you've said to me in a long time."

Her voice hitched, tender and low, sweet and concerned. “But shouldn’t we be…”

Careful? Yes.

Kenzie’s warning was spot-on. Jace *was* traveling into unchartered territory. Places they’d been careful not to go since he’d shown up at the ranch.

And for good reason, too. It was just… with Mackenzie looking at him like she was, softening like she was… Jace couldn’t remember what any of them were.

Chapter Twelve

How long were weddings supposed to last? The reception had been in full swing for an hour and a half, and Mackenzie was as drained as if she'd been moving cattle all day.

"You're not supposed to show up the bride, you know."

Dad approached, smooched her cheek and hugged her. Just like that, all of her strung-tight muscles and nerves from having to be "on" tonight and engage in endless amounts of small talk unraveled.

"Thanks, Dad." His hair had grown grayer since the last time her parents had visited. His mustache, too. The man was the quintessential cowboy. Rugged and strong and dependable. “And thanks a lot for making me laugh at the beginning of the ceremony.” After Dad had given Emma away, he’d turned and flashed a goofy expression at her before retreating to his seat next to Mom.

“I did nothing of the sort.” His attempt at innocence failed and fizzled.

She motioned to her face. “Did you see they put all of this goop on me?”

“You look pretty with it and without it.”

“Well, aren’t you diplomatic today?” She looped her arm through his and watched as the guests mixed and mingled, leaning on him, wondering when she could trade all of this in for a movie and pajamas.

“What’s on your mind, Kenzie-girl?”

She straightened. “What do you mean?”

He glanced sideways at her. “I mean, I know when something is going on with you. And something is. I’m just not sure what. With all of the wedding madness, I haven’t been able to figure it out.” He scanned the wedding guests, landing on

Jace, who was talking to Vera and some other staff members. "Wouldn't have anything to do with a certain bull rider, would it?"

Was she that transparent? "No."

Her dad's low chuckle warmed and comforted.

"Maybe." A golf ball lodged in her throat. "I tried to pretend like everything was okay when he left. That I was happy for him. And I am—was—happy he could chase his dreams. But his leaving broke me, I think. And I'm not sure if I can…" *If I can... What? Get over him? Move on? Let him back in?* All of the above.

Dad patted her hand. "I'm not partial to anyone who hurts my kids. Any of them. Because of course I don't have favorites." He winked at her. "The last thing I want is for you to be hurting, baby girl." The endearment stemmed from when she and Luc had been in the womb—described as baby girl and baby boy—but her brother's nickname hadn't stuck like hers. "I think maybe…" Dad's exhale held sorrow

"...maybe Jace was just a kid doing his best back when he left for the rodeo. His dad sure didn't set much of an example for him."

"True." Victor Hawke had drunk himself into an oblivion for most of Jace's upbringing, and then that same vice had brought about his demise when he'd been killed in a bar fight. Nothing like the childhood Mackenzie had been granted. But her sympathy and compassion for Jace didn't make him safe. "I'm afraid to find out..." *Why he really left.* "I'm just...afraid." A bitter taste swamped her mouth.

"You've never been afraid of anything. As a baby, you climbed everything you could. Finagled a way out of your crib at a year old. I found you on the countertop more than once. You scared the living daylights out of me on more occasions than I can count."

"So you're saying I've turned into a wuss?"

Humor swept over her dad's features. "I'm saying maybe this is important to you for it to matter this much. For it to scare you like this."

A sigh escaped. "I don't like this conversation anymore."

He shifted to face her, his warm, strong hands squeezing her arms. "My girl can tackle anything. That much I do know. Especially with God by your side." He gave her a pointed look—one that said, *Dive all in. Go for it. Grab a little of Vera's mindset and leap.*

After another hug, he left her standing alone. No doubt so that she could follow through and stop chickening out.

His message was right on, and Mackenzie knew it. She could handle the truth with God's help, no matter what it was. And if what Jace had to say was horrible, at least that would give her a reason to steer clear of him, to stop falling for him all over again.

Ever aware of Mackenzie's whereabouts, Jace watched her approach from across the crowd. She beelined for him, and his heart gave a big ole thump in his chest, so loud he was surprised wedding guests didn't turn to see what had caused the ruckus.

Kenzie stopped a step behind him, as if she didn't intend to break up the circle of conversation he was a part of but wanted his attention.

She had it. He eased back from the group, entering the Mackenzie zone that sucked him in like a black hole. "You okay?"

"Can I talk to you for a minute?"

About more work stuff? Why not. "Sure. What's up?"

Skittish. That was what she was, with her eyes flitting this way and that. Her hands wringing. "We might have to talk somewhere else. I'm not sure this is the best spot."

"Okay. Why? What's this about?" Alarm bells clanged, his intuition on high alert.

She released a pent-up breath. "I'm ready to know."

Jace angled his head. "Ready to know what?"

"Why you left the way you did."

Mackenzie's declaration blindsided him like a hoof to the back of his skull. All this time he'd tried to talk to her, to be open and honest with her, and now she wanted to have this conversation here? After he'd basically given up on forcing her to discuss anything regarding their past?

"You want to talk about this now? At your sister's wedding?"

She shrugged. "Why not? Gage and Emma are so enthralled with each other, I'm surprised honey isn't leaking from their pores. They won't notice if we take off for a few minutes." Her eyebrows arched. "Why? Do you need more time? It's not like you have to get your story straight. I want the truth, Hawke. I can handle it."

She might be able to, but what if he couldn't?

When Jace had first tried to tell Mackenzie his reasons, she'd still been white-hot-ember mad at him. Any confession of how much he used to love her would have been safe because neither of them were remotely close to those feelings at that time.

But telling her now that they were getting along… It felt like restarting something they were working very hard not to go anywhere near.

Despite his stumbling earlier tonight, Jace's plans still hadn't changed.

Still…he owed Mackenzie an explanation. So he'd just have to figure out how to be careful with her—with both of them—and speak the truth at the same time.

Two hours later Mackenzie dropped onto the couch in her cabin and used the remote to turn on the TV, then the DVD player. She'd fallen asleep during *Tombstone* the other night, so she cued it up to around the spot she'd dropped off. Not that it mattered. She'd seen the movie so many times she had it memorized.

Earlier her conversation with Jace had stalled before it even had a chance to start, because Boone had interrupted them, panicked.

Mackenzie couldn't decide if she was relieved or annoyed by that.

Probably a bit of both. Relieved that she didn't have to hear the truth, especially if it was hurtful. Annoyed that they hadn't just gotten the whole thing over and done. That she still didn't *know.*

But at some point it would happen. Jace would tell her his whys, and she'd either break or…not break.

Boone had been rattled because he and some of the other staff had been—unbeknownst to Mackenzie—decorating Gage's Jeep Grand Cherokee for the bride and groom's departure.

Someone had decided they should fill the inside with balloons.

Someone had sneaked Gage's key fob from his bag inside the lodge, planning to return it without anyone being the wiser.

And then *someone* had lost the key fob during the decorating.

At first Mackenzie had thought the whole thing was a bunch of drama over nothing. Emma was happy and married, and if she and Gage had to leave in another vehicle, the smitten girl would barely even notice.

But then Mackenzie had realized that Emma's overnight bag was in the locked Jeep. She and Gage were staying at a bed-and-breakfast for the night, and Gage's parents were watching Hudson at his place.

The overnight bag being inside the Jeep turned the situation into a wedding emergency.

Thankfully Emma and Gage had been—and still were—blissfully unaware of the crisis.

Jace, the man who kept surprising her, had taken the lead for finding the key fob.

He'd collected flashlights and directed them all in a methodical manner. And he'd been the one to finally find the fob—which had been buried in the grass underneath the vehicle, near the front-passenger-side tire.

And just as strange as Jace taking over… Mackenzie had let him. Which for her was…big. Like it or not, she was letting him back into her life.

The whole night had left her feeling abnormally emotional.

Coming home to a cabin void of her sparkly, happy sister hadn't helped anything. Emma's things had been moved over to Gage's earlier this week, and now with the snap of her fingers and a marriage certificate, she was gone for good.

Having the two-bedroom cabin all to herself should be more appealing to Mackenzie, but it wasn't. "Buck up, woman. Seriously. You're turning into a whimpering fool."

This sentimental stuff was for the birds.

But even with the changes, for the first time in a long time, Mackenzie still felt comforted. At peace. Her dad's words tonight had hit home for her. *With God by your side.* The short phrase had reminded her that even when she felt alone, she never really was. Sure she'd been left behind a time or two, but never by God. He was her constant. Her strength.

Rap-rap-rap. At the knock on her front door, she jolted upright. Who was still up? And what emergency was she needed for now?

Mackenzie had changed into gray yoga pants and a T-shirt that read Country Roads Take Me Home after the wedding reception, removed the bobby pins, tossed her hair into a ponytail and scrubbed the goop from her face. She might not be ready for another wedding, but she was presentable enough.

She opened the door to find Jace on her step. He had an Angela's pizza box in his hands, and her taste buds clanged like symbols.

He'd changed out of his button-up shirt, crisp jeans and boots into a more casual T-shirt and worn jeans. The earlier outfit… Well, she'd noticed him in it. That was for sure.

This one had the same effect.

The front porch light shone into his eyes, which were full of something Mackenzie couldn't name if she tried.

"What's going on?" Everything from the wedding had been cleaned up. It was late and she was tired.

He shifted from one foot to the other. "We didn't get to have our conversation."

"It's fine. Really. We can another day." Mackenzie didn't have it in her to do this right now.

Jace raised the box. "This is your bribe. We walk and talk, then food. I had to call in a favor to pick it up late. Last pizza they made tonight."

Low blow. She was a sucker for Angela's. And just like he seemed to know and remember all things about her, Jace had her figured out.

"Either get some shoes or you can go barefoot."

Should she claim a headache? Aunt Flo? That second one would really scare him off. Or she could snatch the pizza box out of his hands and slam the door.

Humor surfaced.

"Oh, boy. Do I even want to know what you're thinking?"

"Probably not." The pizza won her over. "Can you put that in the oven on low while I find some shoes?"

"Put it in the oven still in the box?"

"Sure." She was already halfway to her room. "It will be fine. It's just to keep it warm." Mackenzie fumbled through her disorganized shoes. She found one rubber flip-flop, and it took her another thirty seconds to find the other tucked under a boot. She slid them on and walked out to find Jace fiddling with the oven.

"Know what you're doing there, Hawke?"

"Think so."

"You've got it too hot." Mackenzie dialed the knob back.

It was a small appliance because of the lack of space in the cabin, but he'd managed to slide the box inside. "What kind did you get?" The garlic, tomato and other spices were begging her to steal a piece right now.

"Hawaiian."

Her favorite. Of course.

The two of them stepped outside, shutting the door, trapping in the Italian aroma. Dry grass crunched under their steps as Mackenzie inhaled the scent of pine. Rain had been sparse this summer. Not an unusual occurrence for Colorado, but they could use some moisture.

They took the lane that led through the trees and past various empty cabins, small landscape lights casting a warm glow on the path. Everything was quiet. Deserted.

What would Jace confess? That he'd fallen out of love with her and hadn't known how to admit it? Maybe there'd been another girl. Her list of guesses for why he'd left the way he had was long and imaginative.

And about to be answered.

"Did you know that I was supposed to mow the lawn the day Evan was injured?" Jace shuddered at the revelation that had owned him for so long. Nothing like diving right into the past.

Mackenzie's brow puckered, and her footsteps momentarily hesitated. Her head shook slowly as they resumed walking. "No. You never told me that."

"I'd been hanging out with a friend that

morning, and Evan had been working at the feed store. But when I came home, instead of mowing like I was supposed to, I started playing video games." Jace had saved up his money for that stupid game console that he hadn't known would cause so much trouble. "Mom was at work. She wasn't there to nag me, so I let the chore slide. Figured I'd do it later or the next day. When Evan came home, he must have realized I hadn't gotten it done. Instead of hounding me about it, he just…did it. I'm not sure if Mom had asked him to or if he just thought I was skirting it like a little brother. Which I was."

"Oh, J." Mackenzie's fingers brushed against his. And then her hand slid inside his and squeezed. He held on, silently begging her not to let go. He needed her support in order to continue this conversation.

Jace had assumed it would get easier with time, but it hadn't. Maybe it never would.

Mackenzie kept pace and didn't pull away from him as they walked past cabins and pines, the deserted spaces blurring as the regret of that time consumed him.

"Evan mowed for a number of the neighbors, and one of them let him use their riding mower on our lawn. I didn't have permission to borrow the rider, so I would have used the simple push mower. But Evan..." He'd borrowed the monster that had turned on him.

Mackenzie's swift intake of breath was burdened. "I wish you would have said something."

"What would it have mattered? What happened couldn't be changed."

"Maybe. But that's a lot for a kid to bear."

"I was fifteen! I should have known better." Images of his brother in the hospital flared. The flat sheet, the leg that should have continued below his knee but didn't. His brother's eyes, so bloodshot, so panicked.

"Evan had always loved bull riding. He had posters of famous riders in his room. He followed the sport religiously. When he lost that chance... I think it shattered something in him. I know it shattered something in me watching it all happen. Knowing I could have prevented it."

"But—"

"I get that my theory may seem unreasonable." Jace cut her off before she could go on about how illogical it was that he shouldered the blame or believed he could have changed things. "And if it were someone else telling it, I'd be able to say the usual stuff—of course, it's not your fault. Things happen. But emotionally…that just doesn't ring true. The what-ifs and the blame… They've become a part of me, and I don't think they're ever going to let go."

"I want to disagree with you. To repeat the truths you just listed—that you couldn't have changed things, that it's not your fault. But I also get what you're saying. I'm sure I'd be the same way if I were in your shoes."

They followed the lane as it turned toward the barn and corral. "There was a horrible day after the accident, when Evan started tearing apart his room. He ripped down the posters, threw his winning belt buckles against the wall. He basically raged, and I didn't blame him. He slumped against the side of his bed, sprawled out on the floor and pointed at me. Told me to live. To chase his dreams for him. So that's what I did."

Jace stopped to face Mackenzie, and their hands disconnected. He missed her contact instantly. Trees surrounded them, the forest a blanket with the moon and stars sprinkling through. "That's why I left. I had to follow his dreams for him because he couldn't." Unwelcome emotion closed off his windpipe. "I tried to talk to you about competing at the next level a couple of times, but it wasn't easy to bring up the conversation because… I didn't want to leave you. We talked about the future so much. And I wanted that, too. I was torn, confused." He held her gaze, willing her to believe him. "So I took the coward's way out. I left you the note because if I would have tried to say goodbye, I would never have been able to walk away from you."

Her arms had crossed during his speech, and her hands now rubbed up and down her skin, which rippled with goose bumps. She looked to the side, gathering herself, her emotions, maybe even her anger. Jace wasn't sure what all was rolling through that pretty head of hers.

"I didn't think dating long-distance or between rodeos was an option, because I was afraid I'd never commit to bull riding. That I'd always be homesick for you. So I thought it was best to cut all ties."

"Why did you call me? After?"

Those first few weeks rushed back. Jace had been nauseated over leaving. He'd missed Mackenzie with a physical ache he hadn't known was possible. It had been so hard not talking to her, not knowing how she was. Twice he'd tried her, both praying she'd answer and praying she wouldn't. Torn over the need to hear her voice and the need to make a clean enough break that he'd actually find a way to compete, to do well at the sport Evan had loved so much.

"Because I missed you like crazy."

Mackenzie pressed the toe of her flip-flop into the ground and twisted. "I thought…" Storm clouds brewed in her eyes when she lifted her chin. "I always thought you didn't love me anymore and you weren't sure how to tell me."

"Impossible." The word slipped out before Jace could stop it or temper it or downgrade it. They weren't supposed to be entering this territory in the present, but he couldn't lie about the past. "That was never the case. It was the opposite. I loved you so much, but I also *had* to follow Evan's dreams."

Mackenzie had stepped forward, into his space. Her fingertips scooted along his jaw, and Jace's lungs quit on him. Neither of them spoke. Neither moved. Mackenzie just explored him for a minute. Touching his hair, his shoulder, the blank space his cast had recently occupied. He let himself slide hands up her arms and drink in her soft, smooth skin. And then they were kissing. Jace wasn't sure who had started it. He really didn't care about unimportant details like that, because they were wrapped up in each other, her hands looped behind his neck, his raking up her spine. He would swallow her up if he could. Jace's theory and memories of kissing Kenzie… They didn't do the real thing justice in the least.

"Kenzie Rae." He tried to pull back, to be the logic.

"Shut up, J." And then her mouth was on his again, and he was drowning in her. She was all spice and fire and energy. How was a man supposed to resist?

The kiss softened and slowed, and the two of them parted but stayed close, his pulse as dramatic as a teenager.

There'd been a moment at Colby's place when Jace had wondered if Mackenzie had gotten the wrong impression from him. If for some reason she'd begun to think he might not go back to bull riding. Since then, whenever that particular worry had popped up, he'd quickly dismissed it. Of course Mackenzie knew. He'd never led her to think anything else.

But then…why had she kissed him?

"You know I'm leaving, right?" The truth tumbled out, not at all how he'd meant to say it. He'd wanted to be honest, protect her.

By the spark of pain he'd just witnessed, he'd done exactly the opposite.

"I know if you heal, you're leaving again." Her brow furrowed. "But your head, the concussion… I thought…if it doesn't improve, you can't go back to riding."

"It will get better." His hands dropped and formed fists. "It has to. And either way, when I'm done with physical therapy, I'm going back."

Anger, frustration and confusion flitted over Mackenzie's features. "But that's dangerous. You said you wouldn't do anything stupid. Which translates into not going back if your brain hasn't healed. What if you get another concussion on top of this one? What does that mean for your future? What about all of the athletes suffering from CTE?"

"There are risks, yes, but there's no guarantee I'm going to get another head injury. No one knows the future. And even if I do, doctors can't predict how the brain will respond." Though the thought of living with CTE made his saliva take a hike. The disease was torture.

"I don't understand." Mackenzie heaved in a deep breath and pushed it out slowly. "I did some research online." She'd gone from heated to trying for calm. "Did you know there's something called post-concussion syndrome? I wonder if that's what you have going on."

Dr. Sanderson had already said as much. Mackenzie didn't need to go playing doctor or researching his issues. Especially since he was showing improvement.

"I'm getting better. Before last night I'd gone almost two weeks without a migraine."

"But that doesn't mean you should jump back on a bull. I don't get it. Why can't you let this go? What do you have to prove?"

What did he have to prove? Everything.

"Would you give up this ranch?" Jace raised his arms to encompass the place.

"That's different."

"It's not."

"This ranch isn't going to kill me." Mackenzie's volume escalated, and some small animal scrambled in the forest near them, skittering off to safety.

"Bull riding isn't going to kill me either."

Her hands formed a self-hug, protecting. "Actually, you don't know that."

Chapter Thirteen

Three weeks out of his cast, and Jace was doing absolutely everything with his arm. Mackenzie couldn't fathom how that was safe or right or how the man wouldn't reinjure the fracture, but it wasn't her business.

He wasn't her business.

At least he hadn't gone back to bull riding yet. And he was obeying Dr. Sanderson's orders for physical therapy. Jace had gone into town for it twice already this week and had three appointments planned for next that he'd let Mackenzie know about for scheduling purposes.

Tonight he'd participated in the shovel races like a boy who'd been waiting for exactly that all summer. And he probably had been.

If anyone understood the need to compete and play and adventure, it was Mackenzie.

But the changes also meant he was beginning his departure all over again. He'd made it clear that was his plan, and while he hadn't told her a specific date, Mackenzie sensed it was fast approaching.

Now that the twins were home and Luc was back to work full-time, there wasn't as much demand for Jace at Wilder Ranch. They could survive without him.

But Mackenzie didn't want to.

And she hated that. How had she developed feelings for him again? Or had they never gone away? The answers didn't matter. Because Jace was leaving. And nothing she felt about it would change his mind.

Mackenzie certainly wasn't going to try to convince him to be logical and not go. No, sirree.

The man had to figure that out on his own.

Baby screams pierced the darkness as

Mackenzie walked from the corral to the lodge. Luc carted the twins in a double carrier that attached to his chest and back as he paced the gravel path in front of the lodge.

"You been pinching the girls again?"

He laughed, the picture of calm despite the ruckus happening under his nose. "What's Everly doing back there?" He turned so that Mackenzie could peek inside the carrier.

"She's asleep."

He fist pumped. "One down, one to go."

"Want help? I'm no Emma but I can take one."

"It's okay. Cate's in the shower." He spoke over Savannah's continuing cry. "And these two wouldn't settle, so I decided we'd walk until they did."

"Ruby okay?"

"Yeah, she's in bed with white noise blaring so she can hopefully sleep through any late-night interruptions from her sisters. All of a sudden she feels so old compared to these two."

"I thought the same thing yesterday when she came with me on the ride. Never complained once. Maybe I could take her into town Saturday night for ice cream. She's probably feeling a little misplaced with the twins demanding so much attention." Grandpa and Grandma had done their fair share of doting on the girl when they'd been back for Emma's wedding, but now they were gone, and so was Emma. She was at Wilder Ranch for work during the day but quick to scamper home at night to her new husband and baby.

"Ruby would love that. It would make her whole week."

"Consider it done."

Savannah's cry escalated, and Luc bounced up and down. "I hear you, baby. I'm working on it. Now, don't wake your sister while you're at it."

"Savannah Rae, you're going to give us a bad name." Mackenzie rubbed a finger across her niece's cheek. Savannah captured the finger and wrapped her tiny hand around it. Her wail stopped.

"Freeze. Don't move. Don't—" Luc's directions were interrupted by another howl. "Never mind." He grinned. "This one always has a pea under her mattress. Must take after her namesake."

"Ha. Just for that, I'm going to pinch Everly."

His eyes grew wide, laugh lines creasing. "You wouldn't." He backed away, his next words almost drowned out by cries. "I'd better walk with her before she wakes up the whole ranch."

"I'm just turning down the lodge and then I'm headed to bed. Hope the walk works."

"Thanks. Me, too."

Mackenzie checked the offices first. Luc's was locked, and there was no light slipping under the door, but the front office was illuminated like a football field on a Friday night. She grabbed the glass of iced tea she'd left on her desk earlier and cleaned up the condensation it had left behind. Then she flicked off the lights and headed for the kitchen. After loading her glass in the dishwasher, she proceeded to check that the appliances were off. Joe had already put everything to bed, so she did the same for the room and tromped upstairs.

Everything was good there, but on her way back down she heard music. Mackenzie paused at the bottom of the stairs. A sliver of light spilled into black inkiness from the small exercise room at the end of the hall. Her boots clicked lightly as she approached. The room had a handful of machines in it, weights and other items that the occasional guest chose over hiking and exploring Wilder Ranch.

Not that Mackenzie understood that.

She peeked through the crack. Jace balanced in a squat while on an exercise ball. He jumped forward, off the ball, then jumped backward to land on it again, all while staying upright. And then he began to do squats while still on the ball. How was that even possible? She would end up in a cast from one attempt.

"You just going to stalk me out there, or are you planning to come in?"

How had he even noticed her through the narrow gap? She pushed the door open. "Trying to break your neck this time?"

Jace was dressed in workout shorts, tennis shoes and a sleeveless shirt that held a ring of sweat. She didn't recognize the music coming from the speaker hooked up to his phone. He jumped down, walked over, thumbed the volume low.

Mackenzie had done her best to be normal with Jace since their kiss, to tell herself over and over again it had simply been that—a kiss. But no matter how many times she convinced herself, fear kept rising up that it had been about so much more.

Especially after Jace had confessed why he'd left the way he had. That hurt she'd felt for so long had dissipated, and buried feelings for him had sprouted and tumbled out of control.

Stupid.

She should have known better. Mackenzie still wasn't sure what had come over her that night, kissing him like that. And of course he'd thoroughly kissed her back before telling her he was planning to return to riding even if it harmed him.

Even if it killed him.

She wanted to rage at Jace for that, but she was harnessing all of her self-control not to.

He's not mine to worry about.

If only her brain would listen.

He picked up a small metal bar, which had a weight attached by a chain. Arms held straight out, he rolled it up and then down on repeat.

"You come to join me, Wilder? Get in a workout?"

Funny…they'd both switched back to calling each other by their last names over the last three weeks. As if by mutual agreement, they'd tried to separate. To be careful with their feelings for each other. Because yeah, Mackenzie got the impression Jace was fighting the same pull she was.

And that neither of them knew what to do about it.

"I was just shutting things down. Didn't realize you were back here."

"Gotta get in shape if I'm planning to be back for the Miles City Rodeo in two weeks."

"Two weeks?" Oh. She hadn't expected him to go quite that soon. Mackenzie dropped to the wooden bench that lined one wall, a shelf with stacks of small white towels hanging above it. "I thought you'd need more time. More physical therapy."

"Supposed to be six to eight weeks, but I'm going to cut it a little early." Shocking. Why would he make such an unwise decision? Was being at Wilder Ranch—and around her—that horrible? "I talked to Luc about it earlier today," Jace continued. "With him back now, you guys don't have as much need for me. He thinks things will be fine for the short remainder of the summer, after I go."

"Of course. We can handle Wilder Ranch without you." Mackenzie had known he was leaving, and that small blip where she'd wondered if he'd retire hadn't lasted very long, so why did it hurt so much? What was it about Jace that drew her in? Why couldn't she just decide not to want him, to like him, to need him?

"I did the wrangler competitions tonight. And the shovel race." He set the weights on the floor and picked up a jump rope. "Finally. I've been jonesing to all summer." The whirl of the rope joined the quiet music.

"I saw." He'd looked happy and carefree and out of her grasp. "Just don't get hurt on our watch."

"I'm not planning to, boss."

"You probably consider it physical therapy."

"I do." The rope tangled around his feet and he resituated, starting again. "Even got approval from Dr. Sanderson."

Wait. What? "You did?"

"Ah, no." He let the rope go slack and flashed her one of those killer smiles. If they were together, she had no doubt it would be followed up by a smoking kiss. But since they weren't—and since that last lip-lock had been foolish on her part—that most definitely wasn't going to happen.

Because he was leaving her. Again.

Despite everything Jace had told her—about his brother, his reasons for going back to riding, why he'd left the way he had—Mackenzie couldn't shake the wounding that history was repeating itself. That she still wasn't enough of a reason to stay. The future plans they'd once dreamed up together weren't enough either. The man would choose the thrill of riding a two-thousand-pound beast over having her in his life. Again.

Mackenzie didn't even know how Jace's migraines and vertigo had been lately, because she'd stopped asking. And he'd stopped telling her.

After finishing with the jump rope, he switched to a small ball and balanced again, weights in his extended hands. Once his sets were done, he grabbed a towel and dropped to the bench, next to her, leaving space between them. "I stink."

"I noticed." Actually, she hadn't, but his cheeks, crinkling with amusement, made the jab worth it.

Jace scrubbed the towel over his hair, leaving it around his neck. Even with a recent cut, the locks stuck out in a hundred directions at once. "I'm sorry I stayed for the summer. I should have listened to you." He uncapped his water bottle and drank. "You were right."

"Why? Because it was so awful here?"

"No." Those soulful chestnut eyes met hers. "Because it was so good. Wilder Ranch has always felt a little bit like home for me. I basically lived here during the waking hours in high school. Being here has been good for me, but also..."

"Also, what?"

"Hard."

"How so?"

He shrugged. "Because of you."

"All of these compliments are so sweet. Continue."

Jace ignored her sass. “Being around you reminds me of all of the reasons I wanted to be with you when we were younger.”

“But they aren’t enough. They weren’t enough then, and they’re not enough now.” Mackenzie was revealing way too much.

“That’s not true.” Jace tossed the towel into the hamper in the corner. “It’s not about you or me. The rodeo is my job, Kenzie Rae. I have to go back to it.”

“You don’t have to. You’re choosing to.”

Exasperation leaked from his lungs. “Fine. Say it however it makes you feel better.”

“But it doesn’t make me feel better.” She popped up from the bench and began pacing the small space. “This is why I didn’t want you to stay, J. Because this—” she motioned between them “—doesn’t just go away. At least not for me.”

He frowned. “Not for me either.”

Mackenzie ached like the flu had taken over her body. “Then don’t go.” *No.* She’d vowed to stay out of his business. She’d promised herself she would swallow the words and keep her head down and not try to stop Jace from leaving. But the remorse of last time—of how things had ended between them—was too intense. And if her asking prevented that same thing from happening again…she had to try.

"Stay."

Mackenzie's suggestion choked Jace. Never had he wanted to grant her—or himself—anything more. And the fact that the toughest woman he knew had said that to him? Had opened herself up like that?

It slayed him.

"Don't." He dropped his head into his hands, elbows on his knees. "Please don't." His temples throbbed with pain, but not of the migraine variety. This was heartbreak, pure and simple.

"Why not?" Exasperation peppered the question, seeping from Kenzie's pores, sending angry currents bouncing off the walls. "We're just skirting around the truth, and at least this time we get to talk about it."

Ouch. Unlike the last time when he'd abandoned her.

"You could live in town. You could buy a ranch, do what your friend does and train other bull riders. There are so many options. Even if it's not to be with me, then you should be doing this for you. It's time to be done, and I think you know it. You're just fighting it."

She might believe that, but it wasn't true. Not for Jace. There were no other options for him. Bull riding was his life. He loved it. And then there was Evan and all that his brother had missed out on because of his choices, his laziness… Even after so many years, he couldn't let go of that.

"You're wrong." The defense came out strong and confident, neither of which he felt.

"I looked up your last couple years of competition."

That stung. "Why? So you could prove that I'm not good enough anymore?"

"No. I would never do that. But you've been injured numerous times. It's not worth it. Your brother wouldn't want you to do this for him. He wouldn't want you to risk further injury. Have you even asked him? Does he know you carry all of this guilt? That you think his accident was your fault? Because it's not." She crouched in front of him, close. "It was an accident, J. That's all it was."

"It was my fault." Jace erupted from the bench, blowing past her. "And yes, he knows, because he's the one who told me to do this."

Mackenzie groaned and dropped back to the seat. "What did he say to you exactly? Do you remember?"

"No." He couldn't quote Evan's tirade. But he'd never forget the gist. "I was young. I couldn't tell you exactly what he said."

Defiance sparked in her stare. "I think you should ask him."

"And I think you should mind your own business." Jace winced. He was a jerk. He was snapping at Mackenzie for no reason. None of this was her fault. Sure, she was pushing him—trying to get him to consider quitting—but she wasn't the only one on that bandwagon. Dr. Sanderson had expressed the same concerns at Jace's appointment yesterday.

He crossed over, knelt in front of her like she'd done with him. "I'm sorry." Jace laced his fingers through hers. "I didn't mean it. I'm just… I'm a mess. Leaving you was the hardest thing I've ever had to do, and I hate that I'm doing it again." Her sadness slammed into him, rocking him back. What he wouldn't give to make her laugh instead of causing this.

"I hate that you could add another injury on top of not being fully healed. I'm really struggling with that, J."

"I get that. But I just…have to go. I'm sorry."

"I tried so hard not to say any of this to you. But now that it's out, I'm not sure I would have forgiven myself if I hadn't."

There should only be one of them who couldn't forgive themselves, and Jace had already taken the crown.

She disconnected from him physically,

pushing off the bench and scooting around him. "I've got to go. I can't..." She toggled a finger between them. "I can't do this right now. But we're good, okay? We'll be fine until you go."

Liar.

She left the room, and his heart splintered.

So much for not wounding her. So much for doing things differently this time around.

Chapter Fourteen

Jace carried the last bag of his stuff down to his truck and tossed it into the back. It was time for him to get on the road, and anticipation had him jittery.

He'd had his last follow-up with Dr. Sanderson—who wasn't pleased he was cutting short physical therapy on his arm—and Doc Karvina would clear him to compete when he arrived in Miles City. They'd already Skyped, so there should be no surprises there.

His ribs and spleen were good to go. He'd trained hard with his riding arm, and it was holding up nicely. His headaches and vertigo might not be nonexistent, but they were slowing down.

Jace should have gone over to Colby's and ridden one of his bulls before today. He'd told himself he couldn't take more time away from Wilder Ranch, when he was supposed to be helping out, but the truth was, he didn't want to know how his body would react to riding. He'd been clinging to positive thoughts and prayers instead. Choosing to believe he'd have good results and no trouble.

Even if his week had been filled with horrible nightmares that had shouted otherwise.

Luc had returned to working full-time, so Jace didn't have to shoulder guilt about leaving the Wilders in a bind. The ranch was almost to fall season, when things would slow down.

There was nothing else holding Jace here.

Except for Mackenzie. Always Mackenzie.

"Hey, bull rider." Vera walked in his direction. She had on her bright pink tennis shoes and a turquoise shirt along with multicolored shorts. Her arms flailed back and forth like propellers.

"Getting in your workout?" Vera's new lease on life also included a twenty-minute speed walk every day.

"Yep." She paused in front of him, continuing to march in place. "We're going to miss you around here."

"I feel the same." Vera had become one of his favorite people this summer. Her teasing and zest for life were going to leave a hole in his.

"I'll be following your career now, so you'd better make it good."

He laughed. "For you? Anything. How's that doctor of yours?"

"Amazing." She lit up, knocking ten years off her age. "Joe seems to think I'm not too much of a mess in the kitchen, so I'm going to be staying on for the fall season."

"I'm glad you're happy."

"Thanks." Her head quirked, and her

chin-length, reaching-for-silver hair shifted with the movement. "And you? Are you happy?"

"Of course." He was going back to riding, wasn't he? Except…even with that spurring him forward, Jace felt strangely glued to this place, these people. Especially to the woman he still had to find and force himself to say goodbye to one more time.

Vera's arm and leg movements halted. "That was a mighty quick response, bull rider. You might want to think twice before you tear out of here."

The slightest hitch of anger rose up at Vera's intrusion. Everyone had been chiming in with opinions Jace hadn't asked for. Even his mom had questioned the logic of him returning to rodeoing. But just as quickly, his upset dissolved. Vera was in love, and she wanted that for everyone. How could Jace fault her for that?

"Mackenzie's in the barn, by the way."

"How did you know I was looking for her?" Earlier he'd checked in the front office, then Luc's, the rest of the lodge, even her cabin.

No sign of the woman.

But the barn? Was she hiding from him? Or actually working?

Probably the first.

"I saw how much you tried to keep your attraction to each other under wraps this summer. I knew she'd be your final destination before skedaddling out of here today."

Vera could add "truth speaker" to her list of attributes. "It's not worth trying to deny, is it?"

"Nope."

"Mackenzie would be mortified to know that you have us all figured out."

"Then don't tell her…that. Though I'm guessing there's a few other things you could say to her." Oh, boy. Vera leaned closer. "If you could make any choice you wanted to right now, what would it be? The one you're making? Or something different?"

That sitting-in-front-of-the-church-pulpit, being-called-out feeling descended on Jace. "Vera, you should be a life coach. Or a counselor."

"It's not difficult, bull rider. It's just… What would you do if no one held you back? If it wasn't about pleasing someone else? What do you actually want?" She emphasized each syllable of the last sentence.

Kenzie Rae. Bull riding. A time machine to go back and keep my brother from getting injured while covering for me.

All easy peasy, of course.

White teeth flashed as if she'd read his mind, and then she hugged him. "You can do it, bull rider. You're as genuine and strong and good as a person gets."

His throat cinched tighter than a bull rope. Jace didn't say anything more, and Vera didn't require it of him. She was off, limbs swinging, humming to some song in her head.

Jace strode toward the barn, not giving himself the space or time to overthink. This conversation with Mackenzie had to happen. He refused to leave without saying goodbye to her this time. He simply could not repeat that mistake.

He found Mackenzie with Bryce, the vet, who was examining Jethro. The horse had been temperamental lately, and that was a huge liability, since Wilder Ranch horses were counted on to be consistent and cart around new riders each week.

"How's his appetite been?" the vet asked Mackenzie as Jace approached.

"Low. And he's had other gut issues, too." She scrubbed a hand down Jethro's forehead. "But we're going to get you fixed up, boy. You hang in there."

Jace's gut dipped. He'd always been a sucker for Mackenzie's soft side. "Hey, Doc." Bryce greeted him and continued with his examination. Jace sidled up to Mackenzie. "Can I talk to you?"

She kept comforting Jethro and didn't turn to look at him. "I'm busy."

"It will only take a minute." Unfortunately. *Just enough time to say goodbye. Break both of our hearts one more time.*

"Please." His low pleading registered in the plunge of her shoulders.

"I can't." Her wounded whisper cut through him. She couldn't leave the horse? Or she couldn't talk to him? Her storm-cloud eyes flashed with lightning as they met his for the faintest second. "Why don't you leave me a note?"

Frustration ripped from his chest. "Kenz." He kept his voice quiet. "I'm begging. I won't drag you out of here, but we are having this conversation. It can happen right here or somewhere else."

Jace was surprised she didn't respond by stomping on his boot or slugging him. Instead she simply seethed with wordless anger and resignation. "Doc, I'll be back in a minute."

"Okay."

Mackenzie took off like a shot, and Jace followed her into the saddle room.

Once he'd closed the door behind them, she whirled in his direction, all heated upset and impatience. "Fine. I'm here. What do you want, Hawke?"

The smell of leather filled the room, and it brought Jace back to the first day he'd shown up at the ranch and camped out in here while Mackenzie and Luc had discussed his arrival.

Back when he had naively thought he could be around Mackenzie and not love her.

"You're not going to make this easy, are you?"

"You're the one who's not making it easy. You're the one determined to ride when you could seriously injure yourself."

"Kenzie Rae." Her name was heavy on his tongue. Jace *really* didn't want to fight with her. "That's always been the case with bull riding. It's no different this time around." He'd been repeating the same to himself. Only…it felt different. He was equal parts excited and fearful over returning. He might be playing it tough, but he'd give a hefty sum of money not to get hurt again.

Mackenzie had been right—in the last two years, he'd sustained his fair share of injuries. With his recent time off, Jace had buried all of that. But now that he was about to go back, the doubts and fears were clawing their way out of the ground.

Riding scared would no doubt mess with his ability to compete, so Jace had to find a way around it. He had to get back up on that bull.

Mackenzie straightened the saddle next to her, then shifted the oil on the shelf for no apparent reason. "Which bull did you draw?"

"Gnarly."

"What's he like?"

"He's a spinner. Why? You have some coaching advice for me? Or did you just take a sudden interest in my career?"

She rolled her eyes. "I have to do something with all of this jumbled worry and concern that's built up inside me."

"You could trust and pray that I'm going to be okay."

His suggestion was met with a crinkled brow. "I'm working on it."

He was, too.

"You should get out of here. You're going to be behind if you don't take off soon." Her eye contact was sporadic at best. Mostly she was inspecting saddles and the ground. Anything but him.

"I would have left already, but I couldn't find a certain someone."

"The vet's here. I was working!"

"And avoiding."

"No."

"Yes."

She released a pent-up *argh*, with a few extra letters and syllables added on. "This is a fun little argument we're having, but I should get back out there." Her hand snaked out. Patted him on the arm twice. "You have a good drive. Be safe, okay?" And then she pushed past him, as if he was going to let that be their goodbye. As if they didn't mean far more to each other than that.

"No. We're leaving things right this time." Jace caught her arm midstride and tugged her close, wrapping her up tightly. She didn't struggle to break away, and the slightest shiver raced through her. *I love you, Kenzie Rae. Always have. Always will. I'm sorry I have to do this. I'm sorry.* Saying any of it out loud would only wound, so he didn't. Jace just held on.

How was this pain "right"? There was no right in this scenario. Jace had made his decision, and Mackenzie didn't get a say, just like the last time.

She was mad at him about that. She was mad about a lot of things right now. For the past few days, she'd been determined to hold herself together. To survive Jace's departure the second time around. To fight the belief that she wasn't enough of a reason for him to stay. To trust that it was about Evan and not her.

So far she was failing miserably on all counts.

Mackenzie buried her nose in Jace's shirt and inhaled—soap and deodorant and something inexplicably him. Everything about him was comfort.

And everything about him leaving was

torture. A huge part of her had hoped he would just up and leave like the last time. Spare her the pain of this goodbye.

"You need to let go of me." And yet she didn't loosen her hold of him. "Someone is going to come by and find us like this."

Jace laughed as he released her. "Like Trista and Nick? They'd have to write you up."

She pointed. "They'd write you up. I didn't start this."

Jace caught her hand, threading his fingers through hers. Mackenzie's logic screamed that she should untangle from him, but the rest of her wishy-washy self confirmed the truth—it was too late. Too late not to love him again. Too late to save herself.

"You've got some good staff around here. I'm going to miss them and this place."

"They've come far this summer." And a number of them had already asked about returning next year, so they wouldn't have another rebuilding season.

They wouldn't have another summer of Jace either.

Mackenzie was trying to believe that was a good thing. That maybe when Jace left this time, she'd actually be able to let him go for good.

"I'm going to miss you more."

"Stop it. Don't go there." Her head shook, and her heart—it bogged down in her chest, lodging between her ribs, each beat sending out new shards of glass that pricked and bled and tore up her insides. "Now I understand why you left a note last time."

"I'm sorry for leaving." Jace's Adam's apple bobbed. "You could wait for me, you know."

Disbelief flared, irritation turning her skin to flames. "You're going back to rodeoing when I completely disagree with that plan…you're leaving me a second time after I begged you not to stay at the beginning of the summer…and now you want me to wait for you? For how long? Until you can't function? Until you develop

CTE? Until you break something for good or get paralyzed? How long, Jace?"

He didn't have an immediate answer for her tirade. "You're right." His hand scraped the hair at the base of his neck. Where her fingers used to go whenever they pleased. But everything about this man was off-limits. If he was going to injure himself further, she couldn't take part in that. Couldn't support him.

And she definitely couldn't wait. Mackenzie had realized something earlier this week, when she'd been gearing up for him to leave all over again—she'd already been waiting for seven years. Waiting for Jace to come back to her. Waiting to know the truth.

And both of those things had happened, but it wasn't enough. Not unless he chose himself over this sport. Not unless he put aside his guilt over Evan's accident once and for all.

"I can't wait for you, because I'm afraid you'll never return." Not in one piece. Not without the kind of injury that would keep him off a bull forever. Because what else would get the man to quit? He'd already been riding for seven years—and that didn't even include competing in high school. That was a long time. A lot of injuries. "There's nothing wrong with being done, you know. It's not quitting or failing. It's just being smart."

The brown pools of his eyes were mournful. "I can see how you'd think that, but we've already had this discussion. I've already made my decision. I have to go back."

"Fine." Mackenzie crossed her arms, thinking maybe if she did, they would keep her body from crumbling into pieces. "Then go."

A sigh wrenched from Jace, and then he cradled her face with his hands. His eyes held a message, but he didn't speak. Didn't explain or confirm or deny the love written there.

He just kissed her. His lips were familiar and warm and strong, and inside she was breaking into tiny chips of stone. It was the most painful kiss Mackenzie had ever experienced. Her hands itched to reach out and grip his T-shirt, but she fisted them instead. She couldn't hold on to him right now. It hurt too much. Her body smarted and stung in places she hadn't even known existed.

Jace finally let go, and then his departure was swift. He strode out of the saddle room, and she stayed put, unable to move. She waited, picturing him leaving the barn. Jogging over to his truck. Tearing down the ranch drive. Walking out of her life. Leaving her behind. Again.

Five minutes later she was still glued to the same spot, unable to make her boots move, worried her beaten and bruised body was just going to give up and quit on her.

At least if it did, all of this would hurt less.

Chapter Fifteen

Jace parked in front of his mom's house. Another goodbye to check off his list, and he was still reeling from the last one. From seeing Mackenzie so upset and knowing he was the cause. Why had he stayed on at Wilder Ranch?

He should have listened to her from the start. She'd been right. There was no "just friends" when it came to the two of them. He didn't have that button with Kenzie Rae. It was all or nothing.

Jace wanted all of her, but she wanted nothing to do with him if he planned to keep riding. They were at a stalemate.

After knocking on his mom's door, Jace

tried the knob. It twisted in his grip, so he stepped inside. "Mom." His bellow echoed and slammed against the walls of the small living room.

"Back here," she called out from down the hall, appearing a few seconds later in pink-and-green-plaid pajama pants and a robe, her shoulder-length hair disheveled.

"You okay?"

She waved a hand. "I'm fine. Just had a tough night—that's all. You know I have trouble sleeping sometimes." Her lungs clamored for air, the wheezing taking a knife to Jace's already weighted-with-guilt chest. "I'm going to make a cup of tea. Warm liquid usually helps calm things down. Do you want anything?"

It was at least ninety degrees out, so no, Jace didn't. "I'm good, thanks." He followed his mom through the doorway and into the kitchen. Her hands shook ever so slightly as she got out a mug, warmed up water and decided which kind of tea to have.

"Mom, you've got to take better care of

yourself." Jace tempered his scolding with a quiet tone and hopefully some grace he didn't feel. "I've been talking to you about this all summer. It's part of why I came back to Westbend." And now he was leaving and obviously hadn't accomplished anything. Not if her symptoms were still keeping her up at night.

She bobbed the tea bag in the water. "I'm fine, honey. You don't need to worry."

"What has the doctor told you recently? Because I can tell your symptoms are worsening."

"Dr. Sanderson said I'm doing fine. As fine as I can be while fighting this disease. You can call him yourself and ask."

And wasn't that the worst of it? The emphysema had a mind of its own. Jace couldn't prevent it from worsening. He could only push her to slow down, and hope and pray it helped.

Mom opened the fridge and added a squeeze of lemon to her tea. "Are you really going to get after me when you're planning to hightail it out of here and go back to the very thing that injured you?"

She let out a huff. "Jace, I don't think you get to suggest I make changes unless you make some, too."

This was not how he'd wanted this conversation to go. He'd been hoping for *you're right* and *I'll slow down*. "My stuff is different."

Smile cresting, she picked up her tea and patted him lightly on the cheek. "Okay, honey." She moved into the living room and sat on the sofa, and he paced in front of it.

"You could at least quit one of your jobs, Mom."

"Which one? I like both of them."

Jace barely resisted rolling his eyes. "Keep the one that's less stressful and pays you more. Quit the after-hours stocking at the five-and-dime."

She took a sip of tea and shrugged. "I actually like working, Jace. It keeps me busy. Gives me something to live for. People to see. What do you want me to do? Hole up in this house and die?"

Jace was beginning to grow a headache, and this time he had no doubt as to the reason for it. "I want you to live, Mom. Take a walk. Volunteer somewhere, if that makes you happy. But there's no need to continue working two jobs. I've sent you enough money that you shouldn't have to."

She plunked her mug onto the side table and squared her shoulders in his direction. "I've never used any of that money."

"What?"

"I put it aside. It's yours, and I never wanted it. I put it into a separate savings account. It's been earning pretty good interest."

No way. Jace dropped onto the other end of the couch. "The whole point of me sending that money was to alleviate some of your stress." He stopped to swallow, to will his voice down from angry to reasonable. "Allow you to work less. Heal. Give your body a break."

"I know. But I really didn't need it. And it *was* nice having it in case of an emergency. It did provide that comfort for me."

Mom cradled her tea and shifted so that she leaned back against the armrest and faced him on the couch. "I love you for watching out for me. You and Evan both. You're the best sons I could ever ask for. And you're not one thing like your father, either one of you. I'd love to take credit for that, but I'm starting to think it was just the grace of God. That He watched out for and protected you two. Kept you from bad choices. Even with Evan's accident, I can look back and see so many ways that God was in his recovery details. For a long time I thought God had abandoned us. But now I know He didn't."

It was so good to hear his mom talk about God like this. To know she'd found her way back after the hard stuff she'd endured. Jace wasn't sure how to respond about the money, but he did know that.

"I was thinking the money would make a nice down payment on a place for you one day. I thought maybe…maybe you'd come back to Westbend."

Jace had considered buying a place near

Westbend, once or twice over the years. But at the time, coming home with Mackenzie still angry at him hadn't exactly been a draw.

And now he was right back to square one with her.

He winced thinking about how he'd asked her to wait for him. Her reply had been spot-on. For how long? He didn't know. And he shouldn't expect her to sit around, pining for him, after all of this time.

"You don't have to tell me what you do with it. But it's yours. It's there when you need it."

"Fine." What was the point in arguing? "But will you just consider going down to one job? Just...pray about it."

Her eyes crinkled at the corners. "Pulling out the big guns, are ya?"

"Maybe. I'm not saying you have to use the money. But if you do decide to slow down a little, it could still be there as a backup. And you should keep any interest, because that was all you."

Her head shook as her smile grew. “You always were very convincing, even as a kid.” The home phone rang, and she pushed up from the couch, snagging it from the top of the TV cabinet. “It’s your brother.”

“Don’t answer!” Missed calls from Evan had been piling up on Jace’s phone, more so in the last two weeks. “I don’t want him to know I’m here. I don’t want to talk to him.” More like he didn’t want to hear what his brother had to say.

“Are you crazy? Of course I’m answering. He’s usually someplace where he can’t call.” She switched the receiver on and greeted Evan.

Jace stood. He should really get going. Things—like that goodbye to Mackenzie—kept stretching out, taking up extra time. But he couldn’t exactly sneak out while his mom was on the phone, could he?

“He wants to talk to you.” She held out the receiver, and Jace muffled a groan.

How could he say no? The phone was

being jiggled under his nose. Evan could probably hear if he so much as inhaled.

Jace would just have to make it quick. He palmed the receiver. "Hey, E. What's up?"

"Heard you're a big ole mess, little brother." Evan's teasing came through the line clear, and with it a slew of childhood memories. Times his brother had stood up for him. Protected him. Times they'd played army as boys. Rode their bikes until the mountains swallowed the sun.

"Nothing I didn't learn from you." Their exchange felt like home, and Jace's shoulders notched down as his brother's familiar laughter sounded. "Where are you this week?"

"Appalachian Trail. I'm about to take out a group."

"That's great." Evan had found a way up and through his handicap and now led trips for others who were recovering from various traumas. He'd done amazing things with his life, and what did Jace have to show for his own?

Not much at the moment.

"Mom says you're going back to riding and she thinks you shouldn't."

Jace stepped outside and copped a seat on the front step. So much for getting out of town quickly.

"Mom is just overconcerned."

"Really? No one else is? What's your doctor say?"

I'd quit now... I've seen too many lives taken or changed forever by this sport. Jace didn't want to lie, but he also didn't plan to share that information with Evan.

"That bad, huh?"

"No. It's just... He gave me some advice. But you know bull riding. It's a guessing game. I could come back and have my best season yet."

"Or the worst."

"Thanks for the vote of confidence."

"That's not what I meant, and you know it. It's not about you or your skill level. Things just happen in bull riding that are out of your control. What is it that's pulling you back to riding? The money? Competing? Because you don't know what else you'd do? I'll help with Mom if you level with me."

All of the above and more. Discomfort shimmied up Jace's spine.

"And if you can't tell me why you have to go back now, then help me understand why you picked up the sport in the first place. I've always wondered..." Quiet tension expanded. "J, did you start competing because of me?" His brother didn't tiptoe into an awkward conversation; he leaped.

That scene from their childhood flashed back—Evan sprawled out on the floor, his face red with frustration. "You told me to, remember?"

"*I* told you to? When did I ever say something like that?"

"After your accident. You were upset. Tearing down the posters in your room. You told me to live your dreams. To not let anything hold me back."

"Huh. That's not how I remember it."

A golf ball jammed Jace's throat. "How do you remember it?"

"I was angry."

"I've got that part down."

"Grieving a childhood dream. You walked in on your two legs, and I was upset at the thought that you didn't realize what you had. No one really does until it's gone. I may have said something about being thankful for your abilities or chasing your dreams. Or even mine. I'm not sure. But I didn't mean for you to ride bulls because of me. I was still a kid, J. I was mad at the world, and my rampage really didn't have anything to do with you." A sigh rang in his ear. "I'm sure I just wanted you to live, to take advantage of what you had."

The ball of worry slid into his gut and expanded. Evan actually made sense. Jace had never been able to remember the exact words his brother had spoken. Only the way they'd been fired at him. The heat behind them. The guilt he'd felt. Jace had seen the posters, the loss of his brother's dream, and he'd wanted to make that up to him somehow. As if pursuing riding would wipe out his part in what had happened.

"Your accident was my fault, you know."

A beat of silence followed his declaration. "Really? How do you figure that? Did you give the mower a shove?"

"Of course not." Jace swallowed, wishing it would add some moisture to his dry-as-a-bone mouth. "It was my job to mow that day. If I would have done my—"

"Then maybe you would have lost your leg instead of me?"

"I wouldn't have, because I wasn't allowed to use the riding mower."

"Oh, J. I knew it was your job. But you were a kid. I also knew it would take me half the time on the neighbor's mower, so I did it for you. It shouldn't have been a big deal. Dad was such a jerk when we were growing up. Never around and worthless when he was. I probably felt some sense of responsibility regarding you. We're all messed up in our own ways, brother. Just because you didn't mow doesn't make the accident your fault. I'm the one who was completely distracted that day. I'm the one who didn't turn the thing off before checking why it wasn't running right. If I could go back and do things differently, I would, but it happened. I can't change that, and I'm not about to sit at home and cry all day. At least not anymore. I have a life, and I'm living it. Are you living yours? Or are you living mine?"

Yours died on the tip of Jace's tongue. But was that true? He did love bull riding. The sport had become his somewhere along the way.

"I'm not going to tell you to quit," Evan continued.

"You'd be the first, then."

"But just…think before you go back. You've had a great career. There's nothing wrong with retiring before it takes you down for good. I know this sport. I know what it does to guys, how it messes up their bodies. If continuing is about what happened to me in any way, it doesn't need to be. Because you and I… We're good. If there's anyone to blame for my accident, it's me. I knew better than to handle anything the way I did. It was stupid. A fluke. But it wasn't your fault."

Jace's cheeks were damp, his heart pounding as his brother signed off.

After Jace left and the vet finished up, Mackenzie sent her brother a panicked text that she needed a minute—or more like an hour—and escaped.

But her escape wasn't from Wilder Ranch; it was to it.

The earthy smell, the crisp, clean mountain air and hot summer breeze had all unwound her. Going for a ride had, like nothing else would, righted her world.

Mackenzie couldn't give up this place. And if Jace loved riding as much as she loved Wilder Ranch, then it made sense that he couldn't quit that dream. Even for her. Even with his head injury. She should be able to accept that and realize it wasn't about her.

But it felt like it was.

Big-time.

All of these years she'd been wrong—it wasn't the note that had caused the most pain. It was the fact that Jace had left in the first place. Because this round was just as painful. Maybe even more so because she'd realized that she still loved the man.

He was the one. And yet...he couldn't be. Not when he was determined to risk life and limb for a stupid sport. Mackenzie couldn't wrap her brain around that.

She led Buttercup back to the corral and removed her saddle. Sable came to check her out, nosing around her shirt. "I didn't bring you a treat, girl. I'm not your boy. He left us for greener pastures."

The ride had helped, but it hadn't dissolved the wretched war wound of Jace's departure. It was still there, pulsing inside her, cramming her throat.

She needed something good, something pure and full of hope to wash away the encounter she'd had with Jace an hour ago.

God, if You have any comfort to send my way, any wisdom, I'll take it.

Gladly.

"Hey." Luc's voice came from close by.

She turned. "I didn't hear you coming this way."

"Called your name twice."

Oops. Mackenzie exited the corral and placed her saddle on the ground. Luc had Everly with him—her hair was darker and fuller. A good thing since it helped in telling the girls apart.

"Can I hold her?"

"Of course." Luc handed the baby over immediately, and Mackenzie snuggled Everly into her arms like a football. Dark chocolate eyes peered up at her. This would work for something pure and sweet to ease the pain thrumming through her veins.

"I can't get over how much they look like Cate."

Luc's cheeks creased. "And we're all thankful for it." He nudged her saddle with his boot. "How was the ride? Did it work?"

"Fine. Yes and no." She was still drowning, even though there was no water in sight.

"How are you feeling about Jace leaving?"

"Like I don't want to talk about it." Mackenzie stared at Everly's perfect little features instead of her brother. Pink lips formed an O shape and then slid into something close to a smile. Probably gas, but Mackenzie would take it.

"I'm shocked."

A short laugh escaped.

"Are you done being angry at me for hiring him?"

"Nope." If Luc hadn't hired Jace, then her body wouldn't currently be registering at trampled-by-a-herd-of-cattle levels.

"I thought the two of you were finally going to figure things out, make it work. And then you'd owe me forever and ever because it was all my doing."

Mackenzie attempted a smile, the movement slow—like creaky old hinges that barely budged. "You'd like that, wouldn't you? It's hard to be with someone who won't stick around."

"That's what you're upset about? Jace going back to riding? Why? That's his job. Of course he's going to go back."

Mackenzie barely resisted a groan. Men. "I know that. But he had a pretty major head injury when he got here, and it's not fully healed. And I doubt his arm is ready to go either. Partially rehabbed seems to be good enough for him. What if he gets tossed from a bull again? Another concussion right now would cause even more damage. How much more can he take before it affects him forever?"

"I'm assuming you said all of that and he didn't listen."

She nodded.

"Then you tried. He made his decision, even if it is a poor one in your opinion. So why don't you just love him through it? You already do. Might as well let yourself."

Everly made a sweet complaint, so Mackenzie switched the baby to her shoulder and lightly patted her back. "I don't…" What was the point of fighting it? Had she ever not loved Jace? It had been seven years, and no, she'd never fallen out of love with the man the way she'd fallen in. Last time she'd thought he didn't love her back when he left. But this time she knew better.

He'd been keeping his feelings in check, just like she had been.

He'd asked her to wait…and she'd said no. No, because it wasn't convenient for her to live without him in the waiting. No, because she was afraid he'd hurt himself.

She should have said yes.

"Is Jace getting injured again going to change how you feel about him?"

"No." It wasn't. But it could hurt like crazy. "Since when are you such an expert on love?"

"Since I almost lost Cate for the second time, and you didn't let me. You fought me on that, and you were right."

Her mouth bowed, this time fluid, easy. "Wait. Say that again. I was what?"

"You were right. And now I'm right. Because I have never seen you even remotely interested in someone else the way you are with Jace. There are no comparisons, because there hasn't ever been anyone else for you. *Amiright?*"

"Did you just mush that together like a teenager?"

"Yep. Nailed it, too."

"You are such a dork." She didn't want to give Luc the satisfaction of finding his lame joke funny, but humor surfaced.

"Now's when you can admit how right I am."

Not out loud. Definitely not out loud. "Nope." Her eyes were wet, her smile wobbly. And her brother just let it all slide.

He hugged her. "Okay, stubborn." Everly was tucked between them, so Luc left room for her. She twisted her head to figure out what was happening, and Luc pressed a kiss to the baby's hair before letting go, backing up.

"Even if things don't work out with Jace, you've got us, Kenzie. And God. He's consistent. Even when we don't *feel* like He's with us, He still is."

That was the truth that gave her the most hope, the most peace. "Thanks. I'm doing better at remembering that."

Everly fussed and sucked on her hand.

"I should get her back. Think it's time to

feed them. Cate's been sticking to a pretty tight schedule, or we all lose our minds."

Mackenzie handed the bundle over to Luc, immediately missing Everly's comfort and the scent of her fruity baby shampoo.

"Are you going to be all right?"

"I think so." Maybe. Hopefully. Especially if she figured out the answers to a few other questions. Like…did she *really* believe that Jace loved her? That the man had legit reasons holding him captive, making him choose the rodeo over her all over again? And that loving him through this hard time might be one of the best things she'd ever done?

Mackenzie thought maybe yes.

Definitely yes.

"Think you can live without me for a couple of days?"

A knowing grin ignited. She didn't have to explain anything more. Luc understood. "We can probably make that work."

Chapter Sixteen

After the conversation with his brother, Jace could hardly see straight. The highway stretched in front of him, seemingly endless, and he was barely past Denver.

When he'd first started rodeoing, he'd loved the long drives. Anticipation had always burned inside him. Today it was more apprehension.

A word he usually didn't go anywhere near.

But his head—his stupid head—was aching. Would it erupt into more? Or would it calm down? It never really gave him a choice in the matter. Jace popped a pill and took a swig from his coffee cup, using the lukewarm liquid to send what would hopefully bring relief down his throat. He kept his foot heavy on the gas pedal. Heading away from the woman he loved and missed. The desire to call Kenzie, to hear her voice, even though he'd only left her two hours ago, was huge.

He stomped out the idea. He'd done enough damage the second time around, hadn't he? No need to cause more.

Sweat beaded on his skin. It was sweltering today, warming more as the sun rose higher. Jace had both windows open in his truck, and the blistering air swirled around, making a weak attempt to diffuse the heat. He should really get a truck with air-conditioning in it. And he could. But he'd just figured, why not drive the thing until it died?

Jace had done well with bull riding over the years—until the last few bouts with injuries—and after his first year of blowing through his successes, he'd learned his lesson and begun putting chunks away.

And sending some to his mom.

Crazy to think she'd never used a dime of it. No wonder he'd had to hire the painting out on the house when he got back. And the yardwork. The irony of that one stung. The chore that had once been his that he'd failed at. And had again as an adult.

If she wasn't going to use the money, then he'd hire some lawn-maintenance place to take care of things. And maybe get someone on retainer for repairs on the house, too. At least that way he wouldn't feel like such a deadbeat son, leaving her when she was sick.

Sure, she'd been sick for years, but she was getting worse. Anyone could see that.

Would Mackenzie still check on his mom like she used to? Jace's gut said yes. Which only increased the guilt and upset churning in his stomach.

He should be there to check on her.

He should also feel that old eagerness to return to riding growing with each mile that ticked over on his odometer. That jonesing to see the chute, the bull he'd ride, his friends.

But that was sorely lacking today. Mostly he just felt…like he was driving in the wrong direction.

A *bang/hiss* boomed, and the truck lurched and swerved. Jace gripped the steering wheel and tried to combat the careening motion, but he overcompensated to the left. The front of the truck veered and dipped. He must have blown a front tire. The air in his lungs evaporated as he wrestled for control of the vehicle.

He let the truck idle down before tapping lightly on the brakes. Amid more turbulence, he managed to slowly come to a stop, off to the side of the road.

Thankfully no one else had been near him, because he'd traveled into both lanes during the aftermath.

Jace turned on his hazards and made sure he had the space to check out his vehicle without getting run over. Sure enough, the left front tire of the truck was blown. He hadn't checked the tire pressure before leaving town. Must have had a slow leak or something he hadn't realized wrong with it.

Toss some extra hot weather on top and the tire didn't stand a chance. Stupid. That was what he was. He knew better. He'd been taking care of vehicles around their house since he'd started to drive.

"Perfect." He kicked the wreckage. "Just perfect."

Everything was working against him today. He'd left the ranch late because of his goodbye with Mackenzie, and his mom's late because of the conversation with Evan.

He was starting to wonder if he actually wanted to leave at all.

I have to go. At least that was what he'd always believed. But talking with Evan had rocked him, made him deal with things he'd left buried for years.

Evan had known it was Jace's job to mow...and he didn't blame Jace for the accident. He'd extended grace. Would Jace have done the same in his brother's position? He didn't know. He'd like to say he'd do anything for his brother, for his mom, for Kenzie.

But he wasn't staying in Westbend, even though Mom was sick.

And Mackenzie… She'd asked him to stay, to not go back, and he'd refused. She'd pleaded with him to recognize his physical limitations for his own good. For his own health. And he'd refused to listen.

Sun scorched the back of his neck like licking flames, and his skin sizzled.

All of this time he'd dreamed of getting back up on a bull, and now that he was about to, he was petrified that his head would explode with pain and never recover if he did. Or that he'd get tossed and break something else. Something worse this time that couldn't be fixed as easily.

How lame was he? How could he not finish what he'd started now? What he'd been fighting for?

Jace went to the back of his truck and fished out his lug-nut wrench from under his things. He'd start by loosening the lug nuts before raising the truck. His hand curled around the metal wrench just as something hit him on the top of the head.

He looked up. The sky was mostly clear. A few wispy, puffy white clouds dotted the blue. Only one dark cloud held even a remote potential for rain, and it was stationed directly over him like something out of a Charlie Brown cartoon.

"You've got to be kidding me."

He'd thrown his things into the back of the truck because the drive was supposed to be clear. Jace hauled the large duffel, his saddle and a few other items over to the passenger door of the cab and tossed them inside.

More drops joined in, catching him on the back of the neck, the shoulders. He briefly considered getting in the truck to wait it out, but rain was so sporadic in Colorado. If he did, it would probably turn out to be nothing.

He returned to the tire and began working the lug nuts loose. One was so tight he gave up on it and switched to another.

While he worked, the sun beat down and random raindrops pelted him at the same time.

"How is that even possible?" He directed his question to the sky and earned a wet *plunk* in his eye. Jace blinked to clear the moisture away. "All right, all right. I'll stop asking questions."

Traffic had been cruising along at a pretty steady pace while he worked on the tire, and no one had stopped to offer help, which was fine, but Jace heard the slowing of an engine approaching now.

He kept working on the last stubborn nut. Didn't look up until he heard a door open and footsteps crunching.

The woman coming at him was a tall drink of water. *His* tall drink of water. "Kenzie?" He dropped the wrench and popped up from the ground. "What in the world are you doing here?" There was no way she could just be driving past. He'd been headed for Miles City. Last he'd checked, she didn't have any business heading north.

Which could only mean one thing: she was looking for him. The woman either had good news…or something was horribly wrong.

Luc had told Mackenzie not to come back until Sunday morning. Which gave her more than enough time to drive to Jace's rodeo, watch him compete…and tell him she loved him, that she would wait for him—however long it took. And patience was not, by any means, her strongest attribute.

But she'd figure out how to get good at it, because Jace was worth it. Worth that and more.

The words she'd practiced while gunning toward Montana had fled the moment she'd recognized Jace's truck on the side of the road. About the same time she'd begun wondering if God was in the business of orchestrating flat—or more like blown—tires.

"You okay?" Jace closed the gap between them, meeting her by the tailgate and then directing her to the other side of the truck, away from traffic. “Is everyone all right?”

“Everyone is fine.” Mackenzie nodded toward his injured truck. “Just thought maybe you needed a girl to come along and change a tire for you. Wasn’t sure you were capable.”

A wedge split his forehead, questioning, while that grin she loved sparked and grew. “Girls can’t change tires.” His familiar voice, soaked with humor, nestled in her gut, warm and right. Jace reached out and squeezed her arm. “I’m not sure why you’re here…but I’m glad you are.”

“I need to know something before I say my piece.” Her heart was pounding so hard, she was certain it was going to skip right out of her rib cage.

“Okay.” He angled his head. “What do you need to know?”

“Do you love me?” Still? Again? She wasn’t sure what to add onto the end of that.

Jace’s jaw loosened, and he rubbed a

hand across it. His eyes, full of confusion and hope, held on to hers. And then he nodded. "Yeah. I do." He didn't elaborate. And why should he? That was what she'd needed to hear.

"Then I'll wait." He stared at her, mouth gaping. Did she need to be more clear? Fine. "I love you. So if you need to be a big idiot and get yourself hurt, then I'll stand by you while you do it. Because you're it for me. Loving someone else isn't an option. I don't even like other people half the time."

Jace laughed, and man, did he look good doing it, too, with his eyes crinkling at the corners, his smoking smile turning her stomach inside out. "I love you, Kenzie Rae—always have, always will." He kissed her then, burying his fingers in her hair, the scrape of this morning's lack of shave against her lips, moving into her space like he was meant to be exactly there. And he was.

The sky, which had only been sputtering up until now, opened up, pelting them.

Jace grabbed her hand and directed her to the passenger door of his truck, then ushered her inside. Mackenzie scooted over the saddle and other items, and slid behind the steering wheel, leaving Jace room to crawl in behind her. After climbing in, he slammed the creaking door shut and they both cranked the windows up, fighting the sheet of rain flooding the cab.

The driver's window stuck halfway up, and Jace stretched over her. "Here. You've gotta—" He slammed the side of his fist into the door near the handle and then finished the job.

Mackenzie brushed the moisture from her arms, but without a towel, plenty remained. "You really need a new truck, Hawke."

"And *you* really need to stop calling me Hawke. Especially since that's going to be your last name pretty soon, too, and continuing to call me that would just make things confusing and awkward."

Her stomach curled into a warm little ball. "Oh, really?"

"Absolutely." He invaded her personal bubble again—hadn't really left it since reaching over her to get to the window—swooping in for another taste, which she was just fine giving. Jace kept hold of her hand as he eased back from kissing her, and all of her doubts and worries and fears vanished. Whatever came, they'd figure it out together. Mackenzie would start her in-sickness-and-in-health vow now and carry it into forever for this man.

"I was planning to watch you compete. The boss—" she grinned when one of his eyebrows arched "—gave me a couple of days off so that I could drive to Miles City and talk to you. But then I found you stranded on the side of the road." Mackenzie wasn't even going to question how that had come about. And she'd never been happier to see someone have car trouble.

"You like that, don't you? Think you came along to rescue me?"

"I did, didn't I?"

His mouth sported a wry arch. "You did. I have a lug nut I can't get loose. You could probably handle that for me." He sat back against the seat, facing forward, toying with her fingers. "So…"

Had he turned shy all of a sudden? "What?"

"I'm not sure I want to go back anymore."

"Where don't you want to go back to?" Wilder Ranch? Westbend? Montana?

"The rodeo." Jace met her gaze, his earnest, and her heart broke and stitched back together at the same time. "All I can think about is screwing up the rest of my life for this sport." She'd thought the same so many times, but it still killed her that Jace would have to give up something he loved so much. "I talked to Evan. We figured some things out."

"It's about time."

"Kenzie Rae." His head shook, but the twinkle in his eyes told her he wasn't offended by her being…her.

"Evan doesn't remember asking me to live his dreams for him. And I'm sure he's right. He probably didn't. But that was all I could see and hear that day, the only way

I knew to somehow try to make it up to him." Jace smoothed his thumb across her knuckles, making her stomach spin cartwheels the length of a football field. "He told me not to let that dictate what I do anymore. My choices. And I think...*you've* always been my dream. I just never allowed myself to ask and answer that question before. You're what I want." He said it steady and strong and sure. "And the rest? I have to figure out."

"So you're not going to go back? Even this weekend? Not going to compete?"

"Nope. I think I'm going to retire. At least for now. Maybe God will change that for me in the future. But currently? I'm done."

Everything in her erupted in celebration, her nerves tingling, face heating. "I'm so glad. Not that you have to give up something you love, but that you'll be okay."

"Me, too." He kissed her softly. Mackenzie took her time, enjoying every second of the feel of Jace under her fingertips, letting her hands scoot up his arms, which were still damp with rainwater.

Jace tucked a piece of hair behind her ear. "So, you don't have to be back until when?"

"Sunday morning. Why?"

"Any chance you're interested in going to a wedding tomorrow?"

"Whose?" He'd been planning to attend a wedding? How had she missed that detail?

"Ours."

Mackenzie's shoulders straightened. "What? Are you serious?"

"I've never been more serious."

"But..." That was crazy. Right? Except... what else did she want? She already knew from being a spectator and participant in Emma's wedding that all of that fussing wasn't a fit for her. But this man was.

"We could get married tomorrow."

"How does that even work with a marriage license? Can we get one that fast?"

The slow curve of his lips was completely distracting. "Does that mean you're actually considering it?"

"Are you? You'd better not ask if you're thinking about backing out… J." She'd almost said Hawke again.

"Not a chance ever again. You're it for me, and you're never getting rid of me."

"A little stalkerish, but I like it." She couldn't believe she was actually considering marrying him tomorrow. But was that even an option? Mackenzie wasn't exactly up on the how-tos of eloping. "Isn't there a waiting period for a marriage license? Or blood tests?"

"I have no clue." Jace grabbed his phone from its perch on the dash as thunder erupted. This storm had come out of nowhere. "I'll look it up."

They scrolled through the State of Colorado website as Mackenzie tucked her arm through his and leaned against his shoulder. "We'd get the certificate the same day. It says we can marry ourselves after we get the license. We don't even need someone else to do a ceremony."

"What? That's crazy." Mackenzie stole his phone and read. "I'm not sure how I feel about that. I'd like someone to do it. Pastor Higgin would be great, but then we'd have to drive back to Westbend, and not only are we closer to Denver, but if we go home, someone will talk us out of this. And I really don't want that to happen."

"That's my girl."

"We need a judge." She clicked. "But it almost looks like we have to call and schedule it with them. I thought people could just walk in and have a judge marry them. Who knows." She handed the phone back. "We can get the certificate and then ask questions when we're there."

Jace scrolled with the pad of his thumb. "They're open for a few more hours. Want to get it done today?"

Mackenzie should probably be experiencing panic at the idea of marrying Jace tomorrow, but she wasn't. Instead a steady thrum of excitement was racing under her skin. It felt right. He felt right.

And they'd choose each other for the future, just like she'd been quietly choosing him for years. After all she'd never been able to truly kick the man, or the memories of him, to the curb. Keeping him forever only made sense.

"Time's a wastin'. Let's go."

His face lit up, and his lips met hers, swift, sweet, a promise. "I think impatience may be one of your better qualities."

She laughed.

A line jutted through Jace's brow. "I still need to change my tire."

Pouring rain rolled down the windows without interruption and another crack of thunder rumbled.

"Any objections to leaving this—" Mackenzie tapped the dash "—lovely specimen here? We can call roadside assistance and have them change the tire, then swing back for it later."

Jace tugged her into his arms, and she crash-landed against his steady chest as he pressed a kiss to her hair, her forehead, the hollow of her cheek. "No objections from me."

Epilogue

It only seemed fitting that since she'd fallen for Jace Hawke twice, Mackenzie should marry the man twice.

But at least she hadn't been forced to plan the wedding reception at Wilder Ranch that she was about to attend.

Emma, Mom and Cate had seen to that.

When Mackenzie and Jace had returned to Wilder Ranch two months ago with simple wedding bands on their left ring fingers, giddy, unable to stop smiling at each other like lovesick fools and completely delighted with their decision, no one had mustered the heart to be upset with them for very long.

Even her parents had reacted well during the phone call, when she and Jace had spilled the news. Mom had quickly started plans for a reception. She'd asked if they would consider redoing their vows and letting Dad give her away as part of the evening.

Mackenzie hadn't always dreamed of a big wedding, but she had imagined her dad walking her down the aisle. She and Jace had quickly agreed to Mom's requests, though the night could never compete with their actual wedding.

Which, for being thrown together, had been absolutely perfect.

The day Mackenzie and Jace had decided to get married, they'd driven back to Denver, gotten the license, found a judge—the father of one of Jace's buddies. It had all fallen into place. Quick. Easy.

Jace had suggested they find outfits for each other. At first she'd balked. After all, shopping ranked close to hair bows and red lipstick in her world. But he'd convinced her it would be fun, and it shockingly had been.

He'd picked out a dress for her. Simple lines. A sundress, really. An ivory color with a delicate pattern sewed around the neckline and hem. It had spaghetti straps and a crisscross back. And then he'd declared that, most important, she needed new boots. The pair she'd been wearing that day definitely hadn't been fit for a wedding. He'd picked those out, too—camel brown with off-white stitching. It would almost seem as if the man knew her.

Mackenzie had selected new jeans and a button-up shirt for Jace, plus a vest. Because if he was making her wear a dress, she'd required the same level of fancy from him.

And oh, my, had he looked good in the outfit.

Judge Berg had met them at Lookout Mountain Park the next morning, and they'd said their vows outside, with the Rocky Mountains as a backdrop.

Mackenzie would never forget all of the

little details she hadn't expected to remember about that day. Or the man who'd been consistently by her side ever since. They were still praying and figuring out Jace's next career steps. But in the meantime he was helping out at Wilder Ranch again. She secretly hoped he'd stay on. She liked working with him. But whatever he figured out, they'd make it work, because they were stuck with each other now.

"Kenz, you ready to head upstairs?" Jace bellowed from the other side of the lodge's bathroom door. She'd been trying to fix the zipper on her dress, which kept edging open, but she couldn't get the clasp done without help.

She cracked open the door. "And people say romance is dead. Come in here. I need help with my dress zipper."

Jace stepped inside the bathroom with her, shutting the door behind him and letting out a low whistle. "You don't even give anyone else a chance, woman. It should be a crime to look as good as you do."

They were both wearing what they had

chosen for their elopement, and again the man was ad-worthy. He rezipped and clasped the back of her dress in two shakes, and she turned, adjusting his vest, lingering for the faintest of seconds near his abs. Retiring from bull riding hadn't changed his physique, and Mackenzie didn't have any complaints. By the way his brows toggled with amusement, she'd been caught.

"I just got a text they're ready for us." But instead of leaving, Jace wrapped his arms around her, and Mackenzie let herself fall. He felt so good. So right. Warm lips pressed against her neck. "You smell good."

The continued embrace unraveled her muscles one at a time. "You do, too."

"What do you say we get out of here?"

She laughed and eased back. "We already stole the wedding from them. I'm pretty sure we have to give them this."

"True." He gently pressed a kiss to her cheek, as if she was some sort of delicate doll that could easily be broken. "I don't want to muss you up before everything starts."

"You don't have to be so careful with me." Her hair was natural—down in loose waves. "I'm not wearing any makeup but mascara." Which had been her one concession.

"Which stuff is that? The eye goop?"

She nodded.

"That's why your stormy eyes look so striking. It's a good thing you don't wear it all the time. I already have trouble not letting you get your way all day long. Adding makeup when you're already so gorgeous is just unfair."

Warmth flared at the compliment.

Jace's heart was visible in the inky pools of his eyes. "I'm feeling kind of sentimental, being that I get to marry you twice."

"I was thinking the same thing."

The party tonight wasn't huge—family and friends. Most of the summer staff had come back for it, even though it was on a Tuesday. The fall schedule hosted groups every weekend, so a weeknight had been the only option. Jace's mom was present, of course, but Evan couldn't make it, because he was climbing some mountain. He'd sent a gift and expressed how happy he was to see Jace moving on with this new part of his life.

"Well, I suppose we should get up-stairs." Jace's drawl was thick, exaggerated. "Time's a wastin'." Ever since she'd said that line to him in his broken-down truck, it had become a favorite of his.

He started opening the bathroom door, but Mackenzie slammed it shut. "Wait! Check if anyone is out there first. We don't want to be seen coming out of the bathroom at the same time."

Amusement and *are you serious?* warred for dominance in his expression. "You do realize that we're already married, right?"

"Yes. But it's still weird."

His sigh said, *You're crazy, but I still love you*, all in one swollen breath.

He opened the door an inch and made a big show of peeking out. "The coast is clear."

They sneaked out of the bathroom and then headed up the stairs to where her dad was waiting outside the square dance/multipurpose room. They'd opted to have the reception in the simple space, and Emma and Cate had been decorating all day.

Mackenzie was grateful to have two sisters on her team.

"Ready? I think everyone is all set." Her dad held out an arm, and Mackenzie slid her hand through it. "I hope you two were behaving yourselves." Mackenzie knew her dad was teasing, but by the way Jace's face lost all color, he didn't.

"Yes, sir. We were just—"

"Son," Dad interrupted. "I don't want to hear what you were doing. I'm joking. You do realize you're already married, right?"

"Right." Jace visibly relaxed, though his Adam's apple bobbed as if he were trying to swallow a rock.

"I understand why you asked for my blessing to marry my Kenzie-girl after the fact, instead of permission beforehand." Distress pulled Jace's features taut as her dad continued, "I want you to know, I would have deferred to her decision anyway. I trust her. And you. And I couldn't be happier to have gained another son-in-law. I think she picked well for herself."

Jace cleared his throat, no doubt fighting emotion. "Thank you, sir."

"You're part of this family now, son. You've become a Wilder as much as Mackenzie has become a Hawke."

Mackenzie had never been more thankful for her father's wisdom than right now. His gracious, wide-open heart somehow knew exactly what Jace needed to hear. The way her dad had cared for this husband of hers—first as a wounded teenage boy and now as a man—made her cup overflow.

The two men hugged, and then Jace stepped inside the room to stand with Pastor Higgin.

"Thank you, Dad." There weren't enough ways or words to express what his support meant.

"Anytime you need me, I'm here, baby girl. But I'm guessing that won't be as often, since you have a good man by your side."

True. Mackenzie had already noticed how her fears of being forgotten had faded lately. She'd stopped anticipating everyone rushing forward without her and started expecting to be included, in the middle, part of it.

Very Vera-like of her.

The music started, which was their cue. "You Look Good" by Lady Antebellum blared, and Mackenzie laughed. Jace must have arranged the song. She walked in on her dad's steady arm, and he whispered how much he loved her and how proud he was of her before handing her off to Jace.

They repeated their vows, with Jace's adoration and devotion radiating. Pastor Higgin pronounced them husband and wife—again and still—which resulted in laughter and cheers. They ate scrumptious barbecue that Joe had prepared and caught up with friends and family and staff. Mackenzie didn't get to spend much time with her husband throughout the evening, which only made her more thankful they'd gotten married with just the two of them back in August—when they'd been able to focus only on each other.

She was talking to some friends from church later in the evening when Jace approached. "Ladies, I'd like to steal my wife for a dance, if that's okay."

"What?" Mackenzie rocked back in surprise. "You don't dance."

In answer, Jace whirled her into the small area reserved for exactly that—a space Ruby hadn't left all night. She'd been twirling in her flowered dress, and Hudson had been with her for much of the evening, his diapered bottom—in baby dress pants—bouncing to the beat. Her niece and nephew both knew how to boogie when the occasion called for it.

Other couples were already dancing. Mom and Dad. Luc and Cate. Gage and Emma. Even Vera and Dr. Bradley, who were still going strong.

"You don't know everything about me, wife." Jace spun her out and then back, and she stumbled to keep up, mentally and physically. Who was this man? And what had he done with her husband?

"Is that so? And here I thought you told me just a few months ago that you didn't know how to dance."

"I didn't then." He pulled her close, guiding her. "When I found out we were going to have a reception, I learned. I thought you might actually let me lead if I surprised you."

She'd consider being offended if he wasn't so right. Not having a clue where to step next made her totally dependent on Jace directing her.

"And just where and when did you learn to dance?"

His head tipped back, and eyes filled with mirth held hers. "YouTube." She laughed, and his grin edged with mischief. "Actually, Vera taught me."

He tucked her close again, slowing their pace, their cheeks aligning. "It's almost like you don't want to let me go, Mr. Hawke."

"Ding-ding-ding, Mrs. Hawke. You've got me figured out."

Her heart was doing all sorts of mushy things inside her chest. "Thanks for not leaving when I tried to shove you out of here." To think…she could have missed all of this if she'd gotten her way at the start of the summer.

"Thanks for giving me another chance to love you. You're everything I've ever wanted, Kenzie Rae."

Sappy warmth rose up from her toes, cresting her skin along the way. It was almost as if she and Jace were meant to be. Almost as if Someone bigger than them had brought them back together. Almost as if the man holding her planned to be her constant, her forever, her place to belong.

And Mackenzie could get used to that. In fact, she planned to.

* * * * *

Dear Reader,

Thanks for visiting Wilder Ranch for this third book in the Colorado Grooms series. When I started writing this story, Mackenzie and Jace were so frustrated with each other, I wasn't sure how they were ever going to get along. Thankfully it came together, and I figured out who these characters were—what made them tick, fight, laugh and love.

Mackenzie and Jace have wounds, just like each of us. It can be easy to let those past hurts drag us down or define us, but lately I'm learning to do the opposite—to move through the past and into a brighter future. I hope the same for you—that you'll know the great love and healing power of our heavenly Father to stitch up wounds and comfort hearts.

I'd love to stay in touch. Check out my

latest giveaway at Jill-Lynn.com/news, find me on Facebook.com/JillLynnAuthor or visit me on Instagram.com/JillLynnAuthor.

Warmly,
Jill Lynn